Country Coffins

Mysteries by Dale Clark:

Country Coffins

Death Wore Fins

Country
Coffins

DALE CLARK

WILDSIDE PRESS

Country Coffins

Murder holds to life a mirror cracked by violence. At first we see only the crack, like a bolt of lightning frozen on the glass. But the longer we peer, the more clearly we see reflections of our own selves. This is something I began to learn a few minutes past three o'clock of 26 January.

There had been a death at Oak Lake, twenty and some miles from Milquevais. I knew nothing of it, except that Les Jopperman had phoned from Wydota to say a party of fishermen had pulled the body of a girl out of a hole in the lake's ice. I was putting on winter armor—six-buckle galoshes, woolen muffler, topcoat, ski cap, and lined gloves—to go and cover the story, when a voice called from the managing editor's office:

"Ken!"

My name is Kenneth Svederup, and I am the Milquevais *Globe's* courthouse reporter, staff photographer, and all-around utility outfielder.

I crossed the city newsroom (not much of a journey) into Ed's office. It was a smallish room, with a single, frost-furred window looking upon the courthouse square. Ed's desk was littered wrist-deep with papers weighted down by a paste pot and shears and the phone, lying detached from its cradle. Behind the desk stood Ed's swivel chair. Against the wall the Crossway Press news-ticker stuttered details of the latest crisis in Cuba.

The *Globe* belonged to the Crossway chain of Midwestern small-city and county-seat dailies, and above the news-ticker hung an almost mural-sized photograph of H.H. Crossway, the president and founder. For a dozen years the Old Man's granite-jawed, craggy-browed features had frowned from this wall, intimidating a succession of five managing editors. The sixth was expected any day now.

Ed Horace closed the office door, circled behind the desk, and picked up the uncradled phone. In him I saw a veteran of the Crossway system, a man who'd worked on nearly as many papers as Tiger Jones has on Wednesday-night fights. He crowded fifty-five if not sixty, a bald pipe-smoker whose bifocals magnified a mildly schizophrenic stare—a stare acquired from looking over his shoulder at so many H.H. Crossways scowling from so many office walls.

I felt a secret sympathy for Ed Horace; an uneasy identification with him. He was the mirror-image of myself in another thirty years unless, by successfully completing the inevitable newspaperman's novel, I escaped from the Crossway chain gang.

"Long distance for you," said Ed. "San Diego calling, person-to-person. Reversed charges," he added miserably.

But he didn't relinquish the phone, any more than a man with a tail-hold on a bear lets go his grasp.

And for the same reason, I thought. Old H.H. Crossway lived in semiretirement in La Jolla, California, a suburb that is part of San Diego in the sense that the candy bride and groom are part of a wedding cake. H.H. Crossway had the policy of rotating his editors the way a farmer rotates crops. The new man was always expected to better his predecessor's records of circulation, advertising linage, and net profits. If he succeeded, he was given a chance of doing the same on a bigger Crossway paper; if he failed, he got fired.

As I read Ed, he imagined the Old Man on the other end of the wire, about to tell me to take over until Ed's replacement arrived.

Why *me?* Because a couple of years ago, we'd had a murder in Milquevais. The perpetrator of the crime was one Canadian Jones, and by a good guess and better luck I'd caught up with Canadian and got his confession ahead of the sheriff. As a result, I'd been called out to La Jolla and put on a special confidential assignment involving the president and founder's estranged son. So in Ed Horace's book, I was down as the Old Man's fair-haired boy.

I didn't think so, myself. The Old Man blamed the estrangement on his son's friendship with Peter Kelly, and what had I done but meet and marry Pete's sister Clara.

"It's probably Kelly calling," said I, meaning Clara.

Kelly had flown to California to spend Christmas with her widowed mother, and on New Year's Day, while taking down the tree, Mother Kelly had fallen and broken a leg. Kelly was staying out there until the leg came out of its cast and her mother out of her wheel chair.

"Why'd she be calling you at this time of day?" Ed said. "It costs less after six o'clock, and why'd she reverse the charges?"

He knew my salary.

"Maybe she's calling from the hospital," said I. "Maybe the cast came off and the leg has to be broken and set all over again."

I grabbed the phone and told the operator, okay, reverse the charges. And next, over the fifteen hundred miles, I recognized a voice that was neither the Old Man's nor Kelly's.

"Hello, Kenneth?" and hearing, I visualized my mother-in-law, a trim little blue-eyed Irishwoman with black hair turning gray. The voice sounded older than I remembered; it quavered, "Are you there, Kenneth?"

"Yes, I'm here. What's wrong?"

"It's Clara." Mother Kelly faltered into muffled sobs.

My heart did a triple somersault into an empty-swim-pool stomach. It lay paralyzed by visions of traffic accidents, ambulances, hospitals, even mortuaries, as all the way from California, came the sound of Mother Kelly blowing her nose.

"Hello? Hello!" I shouted.

"Hello, Kenneth. I hate to worry you about this, but I have to tell you Clara's in jail."

Across the desk, Ed Horace froze in the act of tamping his pipe bowl, taking it all in. I gave him a grin, not caring. The diving heart had picked itself up, a bit shaken, but back in business. Jail didn't sound too bad compared with the morgue. Particularly because I knew Kelly was incapable of doing anything actually criminal.

"Do you remember meeting Webb and Leah Wilson?" Mother Kelly was saying.

"Vaguely—"

"And Roy Elling?"

"I don't think I ever met him, but wasn't he one of Kelly's old beaus? There was something in her last letter about playing tennis with the Wilsons and Roy."

"The four of them drove down to Tijuana last night," my mother-in-law said. "It's my fault, Kenneth. I urged Clara to go because I felt she needed a change from being my nurse. The Wilsons are *jai alai* fans, and they went to the games. Well, to make a long story short, Roy had a membership card to a private club in Rosarita Beach. It seems he and Clara dropped in there for just a few minutes, and there was a gambling raid, and the police put everyone in jail."

Again my mother-in-law blew her nose.

"It doesn't sound so very serious to me," I said. "The usual thing in a gambling raid is to load everyone in sight into the paddy wagon, but then release the patrons and only hold the operators."

"That may be true in our country, Kenneth, but

Rosarita Beach is in Mexico. It happened last night, and Clara and Roy are still locked up in the Tijuana jail."

There followed a pause, during which Ed Horace played his pipestem across his lower teeth the way a kid runs a stick along a picket fence.

"Have you been in touch with the U.S. consul down there?" I asked into the phone.

"No—I didn't know what to do.'ᴸ

"Kelly's an American citizen. She has rights the American authorities are hired to protect. I'm sure it's just a question of going through the right channels and pulling the proper strings." It occurred to me that Mother Kelly in her cast and wheel chair was in no position to do anything I could not myself do, and more forcefully. I said, "Look, Mother, I'll talk to the consul. The chances are a long-distance call will make a bigger impression. So suppose I buzz him and ring you back. Okay? Then, 'bye for now."

Still gripping the phone in the one gloved hand, I used the other to depress the cradle buttons. "Operator—"

"Just a minute, Ken," said Ed Horace.

I looked at Ed. He ignited his pipe under the flame of a kitchen match, carefully moving the match around to catch all the packed tobacco. He expelled a cloud of sorghum or molasses-flavored smoke.

"I'm going to suggest you let *me* do the phoning, Ken, and you hustle on out to Oak Lake."

Damned if he didn't make it sound like an order, one that pulled his managing-editor's rank on me.

"You filled your ear, didn't you?" I said. "My wife's in a Mexican pokey, and I intend to do something about that first. Oak Lake can wait."

"Why, sure, Ken, I appreciate your personal feelings. But there's two hours' time difference—it's one o'clock on the West Coast, and chances are the consul's out to lunch. It's no use talking to a clerk, and you could be hung up half an hour or an hour, and on the *Globe*'s time."

I glared. "I'm not married to the *Globe*! I am married to Kelly, and no matter how long it takes, I'm going to light a firecracker under the consul."

Ed's pipestem played *tic-tac-toe* across his teeth again. "But you're a newspaperman, and during working hours you ought to be covering the news. Do I have to spell it out—help you draw the line between your job and your personal, strictly private affairs?"

Abruptly I caught on; I saw what Ed was spelling out. I saw it, in fact, in imagined headline type:

MILQUEVAIS WOMAN JAILED IN BORDERTOWN RAID.

My glance flicked away from Ed to the frost-furred window. Through it, dimly, I could see the courthouse, which had been built by old-timers who could remember when the town was just surveyors' stakes planted in the prairie grass. It was old-fashioned, like the old-fashioned monuments that marked the pioneers' graves. Like the old-fashioned cannon on the courthouse lawn, said to have been fired at Gettysburg, which, if fired now, would send its ball crashing into the *Globe* building.

Looking at it, I moistened my lips. I couldn't help thinking of the Milquevais citizens who, over my years on the courthouse beat, had been arrested, had been indicted, who had gone to prison or into bankruptcy. And always with the hope that the newspaper would spread a mantle of silence over their misfortunes. How many times had I gone through the routine of explaining I couldn't do them the favor, that the *Globe* didn't suppress legitimate news?

"Kelly's arrest isn't news?" I threw at Ed what I hoped was a solid, intelligent, let's-face-facts look. "It happened. It's of interest to the whole town. Just because I work on the paper, should I give my wife *and* myself a break I wouldn't give to somebody else?"

He sucked at his pipe. "But if this happened to somebody else, it wouldn't be news—if only because the paper would never hear about it. You've received a personal phone call. Other people don't run to the *Globe* with their family troubles." He puffed, blinking wise-owl eyes behind the bifocals. "You have to be a hero and make it rough on Kelly because you're employed by the paper? Come on, Ken, get going." He walked around the desk and slapped my shoulder, and he wasn't usually a shoulder-slapper. "Those fishermen won't wait forever to be interviewed and photographed, not in this fifteen-below cold."

TWO

I left by the pressroom door, backed the Chevie station wagon out of the parking lot, and, to an accompaniment of threshing tire chains, took Highway 8.

At the town limits stood a signboard: YOU ARE ENTERING MILQUEVAIS—"COTTAGE CHEESE CAPITAL OF THE WORLD." *Drive Carefully—Speed Laws Strictly Enforced*. This sign had been put up for the instruction of tourists, who are mostly amused by it. Cheese is a funny word. So are the pretensions of small towns funny.

The signboard suggests a Gopher Prairie crowned with a chaplet of curds, with whey running out of the municipal ears and a boozy reek of buttermilk on the civic breath.

Cheeseville, U.S.A.!

Well, the tourists who follow Highway 8 to the intersection with Highway 12 are confronted by the glass-brick and plate-glass Farmers Cooperative Creamery, a functional structure designed by a disciple from Taliesin and crammed full of surgically antiseptic stainless-steel equipment for the processing of cottage cheese, butter, and ice cream. There is frequently a traffic tieup, caused by the outgoing and incoming fleet of milk trucks that gather the cow juice from four thousand farms in three counties. A farmer's monthly check may run a hundred to a thousand dollars, and the Co-op's gross runs into the millions.

We have some pastel-tinted telephones in Milquevais, too. And some newer streets lined with three- and four-bedroom houses, topped by television masts that pipe "The Play of the Week" and "Omnibus" into the living and rumpus rooms.

People here—at least, the ones Kelly and I care about—weren't going to think my wife a fallen woman because she'd got picked up in a gambling raid with a man not her husband. In fact, it would be just like Kelly to brag about the adventure, and the raised eyebrows would be because the news had never appeared in the *Globe*.

There's a spirit of uneasy critical sophistication in Cheeseville, U.S.A. The dumbest bozos know an ICBM aimed at the Twin Cities wouldn't have to wobble very much to hit Milquevais instead, and the smart ones are onto themselves in the same way the smarter denizens of Madison Avenue are onto themselves.

I brooded, listening to the tire chains, smelling the anti-freeze stirred up by the car heater, gazing through the windshield at the snow-choked farm fields that resembled a squadron of warships bedded in Arctic ice floes, silos for gun turrets, windmills for radar masts.

On my left, one by one, appeared the lakes.

Milquevais is our big lake, from which the county

and the town take the name. (We pronounce it Milky Way; the word isn't French, but an early Frenchman's corruption of an Indian phrase meaning Turtle Eat Duck.) On the map, the big lake looks like a kite, and the smaller Poplar, Elm, Willow, Plum, and Oak form the kite's tail. All have hilly eastern shore lines, and all peter out into western prairie sloughs, full of rushes and muskrat houses, where the greenwing teals nest and the snapping turtles pull under the fledgling duck.

Today these lakes had two-foot-thick ice covers, dotted with occasional villages of fishing shanties.

I wondered how the Oak Lake girl had died. Winter drownings are usually the result of a careless skater's plunge into a hole in the ice, but the fishing shanties suggested another answer.

Winter fishing begins with the use of a spud. I had a spud in the back of the station wagon. Mine was a five-foot steel bar flattened and whetted to a chisel edge at one end. I'd used it last Saturday to hack a hole in the Milquevais ice. Into this hole I dropped hook and line, attaching the line's other end to a tip-stick contraption to signal when a fish seized the hook. Between bites I'd sat in my Chevie, playing the radio and thinking deep thoughts about my half-written novel.

So I knew that the girl couldn't have drowned in a bait fisherman's merely hat-sized hole. But spear fishing was different. A spear fisherman stays in his shanty with a kerosene lantern that's more for warmth than for illumination. He hacks a large hole in the ice, and into it dumps a grain sack of shelled corn. The kernels sink to the bottom and there create a patch of brightness. Spear at the ready, the fisherman waits until an investigating northern swims into range.

I guessed a skater or hiker *could* drown in a spear fisher's hole if the shanty had been moved away, if the ice had not refrozen before the victim came along, if it happened after dark. There would have been a sudden splash, a flooding of water over the ice around the hole, and a brief, frantic struggle in the paralyzingly cold water.

It seemed a hell of a way to die, but also it helped me muse that there are worse fates than being locked up overnight in a jail, even a Tijuana jail.

The miles ticked away. The village of Wydota loomed up, at first as a water tower and a pair of grain elevators etched on the horizon, becoming a wider stretch of paving lined with gas stations, a farm-implement store, the usual prairie-town array of frame and brick store fronts. Six hundred and four persons lived here, or say two hundred families, of whom a hundred and eighty-seven were *Globe* subscribers—all on account of Leslie Jopperman, the local railroad, express, and telegraph agent, who was the *Globe*'s Wydota correspondent in his spare time.

The paper had a dozen hamlet and rural-township correspondents; typically, they were middle-aged women contributing items about who Sunday-dinnered with whom, and who motored to the Twin Cities when. They were country-society reporters who wouldn't see the news value in a burning house unless the Ladies Aid was there serving coffee and doughnuts to the firemen.

Les Jopperman was different. He was a man, for one thing, and he had creative literary talent. I knew Les as a member of the Thursday Pen Club, which meets in the Milquevais Public Library under the tutelage of Miss Florrie Schultz. Les was the only one of us making any real money out of his writing. He wasted no time on novels or magazine love stories or pseudo-scientific thrillers. No, he specialized in twenty-five-word slogans; he specialized in contests and got paid off in clocks, radios, automatic washing machines, and once, a $2500 second prize for an essay on Why I Feed My Family Exploded Oats.

He was unmarried, batching in housekeeping rooms over the Mud Hen station, within earshot of the telegraph key.

I steered the Chevie across the railroad tracks and braked next to a blue and white Co-op milk truck parked at the red-brick platform. The wind struck me a Siberian blast, as if since I'd left Milquevais the North Pole had slipped a thousand miles southward. The station building ahead wore the customary coat of railroad red paint (they must mix soot in with the pigment). In one of the Jack-frosted windowpanes of the waiting room glimmered a yellow oblong. I stopped to consult the thermometer nailed to the window sash: "Minus-eighteen degrees." I looked up; the yellow oblong had vanished. I hurried on into the waiting room, into a past-century setting having as its centerpiece a head-high, fat-bellied coal stove.

Warming his hands at the stove was the milk-truck driver, a wiry, sandy-haired chap wearing the Co-op blue winter coat over dairy-white coveralls.

You'd think a newspaperman would know everyone in Milquevais. But the creamery drivers spend their days on the country roads, while I work evenings in the newsroom. The *Globe* is a morning paper, and goes to press at 10 P.M. in order to get the bundles onto the midnight northbound for Goodlands and Hay Center.

I gave the barely familiar face a nod. In return, it nodded. I swung to the ticket window, bracketed between a gum-dispensing machine and a blackboard bulletin of train times. The window was closed, but from behind it sounded the telegraph key.

"Les?" called I.

"He's out someplace."

I glanced at the driver, and it now dawned on me who he was. More exactly, it dawned on me whose husband he was.

It is part of my job to attend the Co-op's quarterly and annual board meetings, and thus I had met Jessica Riker. She worked in the business office and had a husband who bowled on the Co-op's championship team; in fact, six or eight weeks ago I had snapped the team picture for the sports page. The name flashed up—Ralph Riker.

"I've been waiting fifteen minutes myself," Ralph Riker said. "I've got this shipment for the five-o'clock southbound."

The shipment lay upon the waiting-room bench; a

large paper-wrapped bundle, securely tied with binder twine, dangling a pasteboard Express tag. It seemed to me that I detected in the air a faintly gamy odor, a little like the sniff of a skunk across a forty-acre field.

"Leslie may have gone out to Oak Lake," I said.

"On a day like this?"

"He called the paper about a girl's body being pulled out of a hole in the ice."

A moment passed. Then Ralph Riker said, "Who was she?" His voice had changed—not very much, but enough that I looked sharply into his face.

From the cold, his face had the weathered gray-red complexion of a field beet. Otherwise, it was the face of what the girls call a "nice-looking fella"—neatly chiseled features unspoiled by any evidences of intellectual profundity or undue emotional sensitivity. He did not look like a nervous fella. But his voice had certainly been nervous.

"I don't know," I told him. "Les didn't say who she was, and I doubt if he knew. I imagine he'd just heard of it, the way you hear there's been an accident down the road without being told who's hurt."

Several moments passed. The odor of skunk in the waiting room grew slightly yet perceptibly stronger. I supposed the shipment was warming.

"The Busch brothers are seining the lake," Riker said. "It must of been them found her."

"You couldn't prove it by me."

"It's funny the Busches wouldn't know. Wydota isn't such a metroplis that a person could disappear and not even be missed until the body was pulled out of the lake."

"She might not have been missing very long, however," said I. "She may have just skated into the hole, and they didn't get to her in time."

"Sure, but you'd think the Busches would know who she was."

"Well, Ralph, I'll find out for you if I can. You can read all about it in tomorrow's paper."

He stared at the stove, not at me. "It's in my territory, you know. I go to practically all the farms around the lake, and she may be somebody I know."

This is what you get for accusing the other fellow of nosey curiosity, and what could I say? I wanted to make amends.

"It could be you're right," I said. "Anyway, I'm going out there, and I expect I'll run into Les. So if you like, I'll take your package and give it to him—save you hanging around here any longer."

"Well, thanks, but I guess not. It can go tomorrow just as well." Riker suddenly stepped in front of me and dropped to one knee in front of the ticket office's Dutch door. I saw the corner of an oblong yellow envelope under the door. Riker pulled it out, picked it up, peered at the face.

"*Kenny Svederup*. Les must have left it for you. I didn't notice before, did you?"

This time his voice was perfectly normal, and yet I knew he had been examining this envelope at the window, trying to read its contents by transmitted light. He had obviously got it tucked back under the door while I paused to read the thermometer.

"Why don't you open it—maybe it says when he's due back."

I tore open the envelope and found a telegram flimsy overscrawled with Leslie Jopperman's idelibly penciled, eccentric handwriting. *Dear Kenny,* he began (and nobody but Les ever calls me Kenny), *'tis 'Murder most foul, strange, and unnatural.' But as I'm not employed by the county, and am by the Globe, I've taken the journalist's prerogative of first calling the paper. Now I suggest you ring up Sheriff Popke and proceed posthaste ahead of him. You see, I've acted to protect the "scoop."*

Below, Leslie had appended a short-cut map. There was no signature, nor any need of one.

THREE

Leslie Jopperman's map put me on a graveled county road following the curve of the Mud Hen tracks. The rails were laid atop an eight-foot embankment, for in the eighties, when the branch line came up from Indian Rock through Wydota and Milquevais, much of the country had been undrained prairie bog.

Next, the map switched me onto a dirt township road. I was thinking over Les's note, first of all the last word in it. Les knew the *Globe* did not publish extras; not until six in the morning would the paper begin landing on front porches; so how could the half-hour headstart on Sheriff Popke result in a "scoop"?

I said to myself that a small-town newspaper can never really be first with the tidings of local crimes and catastrophes; town-talk grapevine and rural party lines spread the news too fast. What a good small paper can do is be the first with the sober second look. The *Globe* is worth its price because when you've read it, you know how much you've already heard is true and how much is magnified rumor and exaggerated gossip.

And there I came full circle to the problem of Kelly in jail.

If I honestly believed in sober, responsible, factual

news reporting, why was I so willing to accept the favor from Ed Horace?

I might have said, "Let's face it, Ed. The truth has a habit of leaking out. And if this story ever gets spread around by word of mouth, it'll look as if you and I covered up something shameful and disgraceful about my wife. I'm in favor of going ahead and printing the facts."

I could still say so. Any time up until the *Globe* went to press tonight, I could say so. Only, I didn't want to. My wife had been arrested while dating with another man, and I didn't want to hold that fact up to the light for people to read meanings into.

Obeying the map, I turned the Chevie off the dirt road and across a lowered barb-wire fence where a truck trail climbed the slope of a snow-plugged cornfield.

October's premature blizzard had caught a good many fields unharvested. A farmer can't haul a mechanical picker through hip-deep drifts, and here the brown stalks stood dripping their unhusked ears into the snowbanks.

It set a royal table for the wildlife. From in front of the station wagon's left front fender, a cock pheasant exploded into flight and left a string of raucous curses as he flew ahead over the hilltop. Our pheasants are immigrants, imported to replace the prairie chickens whose drumming used to reverberate in the twilights. This one's *yackety-yak* roused a jack rabbit, which loped across the field in coil-spring ten-yard bounds. The jacks had been here before the Indians.

Pheasant and jack rabbits both were sights to gladden the dreary sub-zero afternoon, and there's nothing like the outdoors to snap a man out of the introspective fantads.

The Chevie bumped over the slope's rise and began jolting downhill toward Oak Lake. There spread before me a winter scene etched in black-browns and gray-whites—a low-sweeping shore line marked by a straggling row of bare-branched willow and cottonwood. (The oak trees at Oak Lake are on the east shore, where the '55 twister smashed a dance pavilion and made matchwood of half the summer cottages.)

Out past the shore line began a belt of slough grass and cattail, dotted with muskrat mounds and drifted full of snow that had blown in off the lake's bare ice.

The truck trail crossed this belt, and up close I noticed suspicious brown pockings on the snow-capped muskrat houses. The muskrat is no rat. Anatomically, an oversized aquatic field mouse, it is trapped for its fur, and trapped most easily by illegally chopping into the houses and placing Victor No. 2's on the feeding shelves. It looked to me as if somebody had been chopping divots from these houses—the escaping warmth would explain the brown spots. It might have been mink, though—they tunnel into the lodges.

Life in the country has its savage side, not just survival-of-the-fittest savagery, either. Man is the worst. For every duck dragged down and eaten by the snapping turtles, probably a hundred birds die of lead poisoning from gobbling down the pellets fired from shotguns.

Ahead of me, out on the ice, was a huddle made up of parked cars, a tarpaulin-covered truck, a stack of wooden boxes piled to form a windbreak for a group of sheepskin-coated, hip-booted fishermen.

This was the winter seining operation. A lake is seined under ice simply enough. The fishing crew spud a series of holes through the ice, then pole a rope from hole to hole under the ice. Over the rope they pull the fish net. Finally, they hitch a tractor or truck onto the seine and make the haul through a larger hole in the ice.

One car, a coupe, stood parked apart from the others. Its door was hinged open, and Leslie Jopperman clambered out to wigwag me to a stop.

Les was a plump little guy, wearing a brakeman's ear-flap cap and a raccoon coat like in a John Held, Jr., drawing—a costume that left visible a face curiously resembling that of a middle-aging kewpie doll.

Along with a biting sample of the winter wind, Les got into the seat beside me.

"Kenny, what would you say if I told you fate has put us in the way of a jackpot, and with any luck we should make ourselves a nice tidy $1000?"

"I'd say what the hell are you talking about?"

"And I'll answer you from the beginning, Kenny. The story starts with the arrival of a telegram addressed to Earl Bowers—you know, the game warden.

It seems Mrs. Bowers has presented him with a bouncing eight-pound four-ounce son. She's in a hospital in the Cities. They expected complications—something to do with the RH factor. I thought Bowers would want to know it turned out okay. I knew he was out here with the fishing gang, but I had no way of phoning him, so I drove out with the telegram. And reached the scene practically as they were fishing this girl's body in the seine."

"What girl? Who is she?"

"That's part of the mystery, but let me tell you this *my* way. The Busches were all for loading the body onto the truck and starting for town. I forestalled that by pointing out there's a law against transporting corpses and legally one must wait on the authorities before touching anything on the scene of a violent death. I said I'd drive to town and notify the sheriff. Actually, the truth is, I had instantly perceived the **financial possibilities**."

On Leslie Jopperman's face was the expression of an Eskimo stalking a fat seal or a polar bear.

"What do you mean?" said I.

"I mean the possibility of entering this body in a contest."

"You kidding? Or are you crazy?"

"Well, I mean *Bloody Murder Magazine* is offering a $1000 first prize for the best unpublished real-life murder case submitted by its readers."

"How many coffin lids does it take to enter the contest?"

Les regarded me reproachfully; he appreciated only his own brand of comedy.

"I'm serious," said he. "I'm going to suggest a collaboration, Kenny. You do the legwork and take the pictures, and I'll do the literary chore of preparing the entry. Any prize we win we'll split fifty-fifty."

This I thought a very strange proposition. Suppose that a murder had occurred? Suppose it were a murder spiced with sex and salted with enough violence to gratify the taste of a true-crime magazine? If so, I and not Leslie Jopperman had the courthouse beat— the ringside ticket to the investigation. If the case were to be written up for a magazine, why should I not write it? Why should I go halves with Les?

There was a reason, really. I'd never finish my novel if I started spending my spare time entering contests of any kind.

"What's the big hurry, Les?" said I. "That kind of magazine publishes only solved murders. They'd want a court conviction as insurance against libel suits. Even if this *is* murder, it'll be weeks and maybe months before the case goes to a jury."

"We can't wait for that!" cried Leslie.

"Why not?"

"I'll tell you why." A grimace of feverish energy dented the mouth corners into Les's kewpie cheeks. "I've studied the product, as I always do before tackling a contest. And I know what *Bloody Murder Magazine* wants and will pay $1000 to get. Art!"

"Art?"

"Certainly. They run those horrendous stories, and what do they print as illustrations?" He laughed contemptuously. "An amateur snapshot of the victim. A posed photo of a cop pointing at the shallow grave where the body was found. I swear this contest can be won by mailing in a story plus a photographic documentary of pictures showing the step-by-step phases of the official investigation."

My nod paid tribute to Leslie Jopperman's cleverness. I myself would never have thought of this angle.

"Now you know why I wanted you here ahead of the sheriff, Kenny. So we could work out our deal before the investigation starts."

I reached for the leather case containing my Speed Graphic and its accessories. I thrust a filmholder into the springback and popped a bulb into the flash-gun. There could be no harm in exposing a few films. I stood to lose nothing if the "murder" proved to be suicide or an accidental drowning.

"Shake on it?" questioned Les.

"Let's put it I'm keeping an open mind," I said.

"All right, Kenny. Then I'll tell you what I think will make a dilly of a magazine illustration, and that's a candid shot of the victim being lifted out of the hole in the ice."

I stared. "You mean she's still in the water?"

"Of course not, Kenny. The body's laid out under the truck tarp over there. But I'm confident you can talk the fellows into slipping it back into the lake—just a quick dip, long enough for you to snap the picture."

I started to laugh, but the laugh never got past my tonsils, for I saw that Leslie Jopperman was entirely serious. He was clever, yes, only the cleverness was flawed.

I stepped out onto the ice. The wind blowing across Oak Lake was full of invisible needles. I hurried around into the quiet zone behind the packing-box barricade.

Here the work crew, all breathing like tea kettles, worked with dip nets at their seining hole.

Commercial fishermen may take only rough fish; the northern and wall-eyed pike, they were returning unharmed to the water. The carp, though, were being tossed up onto the ice, and I picked my path through these handsome, full-bodied, delicately armored creatures. The carp is not a native fish; the first were stocked from Europe about the time the Mud Hen tracks were laid, and like the rabbit in Australia, they have multiplied and become a pest. They are said to be edible, provided the cook takes the trouble to remove the strip of black back fat, but I never knew any Milquevais resident hard up enough to make his dinner on carp. The commercial catch is shipped to the cities, and there eaten by "foreigners" or maybe manufactured into catfood.

I stepped up to Game Warden Bowers, a big man made bigger by Arctic coveralls. He was tallying the returned game fish as a basis of estimating the lake's population.

"Hi, Earl."

" 'Lo, Ken."

I sensed something conspiratorial in the game warden's manner.

"Hell of a thing happened here, huh?" I said.

"It's a nuisance to me personally. I want to finish up, and not be tied up in a lot of rigamarole," said Bowers. "My wife's had a baby. I promised to take a couple days off to be with her when the kid came."

They all wanted to finish the job, of course, and the work went on in dour concentration.

I'd never before covered a story in which the witnesses were too busy to speak to a reporter; the trouble usually was to keep them from all talking at once. An aura of hostility hung over the scene. I could feel eyes at my back as I stepped to the truck and loosened the tarpaulin ropes.

I lifted the tarp, and it ballooned full of wind. I peered in at the Oak Lake victim.

The body on the truck bed lay clad in a swimsuit, a one-piece garment made of Lastex-like fabric having a white background splashed with a design of blue, stylized, vaguely Hawaiian flowers.

She had a blonde ponytail, which looked more like frayed copper wire than human hair.

Certain physiological changes occur when a body is long immersed in water, and these changes had occurred. The face could not have been recognized by the victim's own mother or closest friend.

In warm weather, I might have guessed the girl had been in the lake two or three days. Under the Oak Lake ice, the time might have been two or three weeks.

Leslie Jopperman stood at my shoulder. "A bathing suit in January! It has to be murder, Kenny. She didn't go for a swim and accidentally drown in the middle of winter."

"It looks that way, all right."

"The bathing suit is a clue," said Les. "Obviously, the killer expected the body couldn't turn up before next spring at the earliest, and then the bathing suit would make everyone think this girl drowned last summer. It's the work of a macabre genius, and you have to admire the talent and ingenuity. He just didn't know about the seining holes."

I saw nothing to admire in this evidence of brutal, vicious villainy. But I had caught onto the fishing gang's glum silence. They'd lifted the body onto the truck and covered it with the tarpaulin because what you normally do with bodies is lay them out and cover them up. In this case, it had been a mistake. For now the victim lay frozen fast to the truck floorboards.

FOUR

It grew colder still as blackening winter twilight descended upon Oak Lake. The trees of the shore line merged into the sooted sky. Here and there on the surrounding prairie appeared farmhouse lights, looking as distant as Arcturus. On the truck, under the tarpaulin shroud, the girl's body went on turning into something like cast-iron statuary.

Leslie Jopperman had headed his coupe toward Wydota, in order to reach the station ahead of the five o'clock southbound.

The fishing crew knocked off work. I lined them up for a flash group photo—left to right, Norman and Henry Busch, John Hetzmier, Enoch Larsen, Alfred Albrecht, Harvey Staples. They were a little worried whether the carp would be condemned because it was taken from water that contained a corpse. Les hoped to turn a profit from the dead girl; the Busch Brothers feared to take a loss on her. Earl Bowers presumably brooded about his new-born son, and my own thoughts turned to Kelly in the Tijuana jail.

At last, across the ice from the east shore, advanced flashing headlights. Up pulled the county sedan, and out stepped Sheriff Willie Popke. He had stopped to pick up Coroner Soole, and they had traveled by Highway 12 down the lakes' east shores.

Willie Popke had been, in his younger years, a semi-pro catcher, good enough in his youth to have had a tryout with the Milwaukee club when the Brewers were a Triple-A team. Failing to make the grade, Willie had been speed cop in Milquevais and next chief of police, after which he'd run for sheriff because he needed the salary. He was as bright as the average big-city police sergeant, and maybe as bright as a lot of police captains.

It just happened there wasn't anything any cop could do with a frozen corpse in the dark and the twenty-below cold. Popke told the Busch Brothers to drive their truck into the Ford Garage in Milquevais: "—twenty miles an hour, and slow down to ten on the curves. There might be broken bones. We don't want it claimed they got broke while you hauled her."

I snapped a picture of Game Warden Bowers pointing out the hole in the ice to Sheriff Popke and the toothpick-thin coroner.

The Busches started their truck across the lake, taking Highway 12 instead of jolting their burden through the cornfield. The game warden drove off the same way. The fishing crew piled into another car and headed in the direction of Wydota.

The sheriff, the coroner, and I sat awhile in the county sedan—they in front, I in the back seat. Willie Popke bit the tip from a rum-soaked crook and set it going with the dashboard lighter.

"We're looking for a dame who dropped out of circulation a couple, three weeks ago," said Willie, "and no missing person report to go on. So her disappearance wasn't reported. It could be one of those deals where a guy conks his missus and tells the neighbors she's gone visiting her folks. Like Ken here says his wife is in California, but nobody knows, and we're only taking his word."

"Svederup's wife isn't a blonde," said Doc Soole.

"I don't say this is his wife's body. I say she could be somebody's wife and the neighbors could think she's just away visiting. They can read in the paper the body has been found, and they won't make the connection unless you needle them into suspecting. Ken knows how to word it."

"Sheriff William Popke theorizes the victim may be a local woman whose absence from her home has not been reported. That your statement?"

"You could make it stronger."

"What's her description, then?" said I. "Was she five feet three or five feet six? Weigh one-ten or one-thirty? Was she a girl of eighteen or a woman of twenty-eight?"

"That's Doc's department. Doc?"

"All this will take time," said Coroner Soole. "The body will have to be thawed off the truck, and then I don't expect to open it up and find a photostated birth certificate. The determination of age depends on the progress of ossification of the skeletal processes, particularly the fusion of certain vetebrae."

"When can you give me a statement?" I asked.

"How can I tell? Eleven o'clock, perhaps midnight."

"I can't promise Ed Horace will hold the paper," I said. "It isn't a national election, and overtime in the shop costs money."

The sheriff chewed on his cigar. "Yeah, but soon's it comes out the body's found, the killer's going to start covering his tracks. I say don't let's all stand around looking at the seams on the ball while the guy steals second base!"

We broke it up.

Getting back in the Chevie was like taking a seat in a deep-freeze box. I started the motor and put the heater to work, removed the filmholder from the camera, and stored them both in the leather case. Meanwhile, the sheriff's sedan followed its gleaming headlight across the ice.

Second thoughts occurred. Milquevais County is predominantly Scandinavian. Four in ten women are blondes, four in ten of the younger ones wear ponytails. Two or three weeks ago, several hundred girls had been returning to universities and colleges from the holidays. The Globe ought not terrify half the parents into supposing that the Oak Lake victim was their daughter.

I watched the five o'clock southbound draw a string of coach windows around the basin of Oak Lake in the direction of Indian Rock. In the old, wet years the lake waters sometimes used to inundate the tracks; hence the Mud Hen nickname.

Looking after the Mud Hen's vanishing lights, I

mused that maybe the dead girl had lived down around Indian Rock, in Baxter County. In that case, publishing her description in the *Globe* wouldn't help any, for the paper hadn't Baxter County circulation.

Looking after the Mud Hen, I became suddenly aware of a twinkle of stationary light—not from a farmhouse, but apparently shining out of one of the summer cottages on the lake shore.

That seemed odd.

The summer cottages around our lakes are shacky affairs, occupied from June to Labor Day by cityfolk who can't afford more expensive and distant Northwoods vacations. In winter a cottage would be about as cozy as a woodshed unless somebody had used insulation and weatherstripping and storm sash to convert it into a year-round dwelling.

The light narrowed into nothingness; it had shone through a door, now closed.

My thoughts leaped away in jack-rabbit bounds: A murderer burying a body under lake ice would pretty surely work at night. His light would be highly visible to a cottager. Even if he showed no light, the ringing blows of a steel spud could be heard a long ways.

If a cottage was occupied, the occupant might remember and be able to pinpoint the date—

I shifted gears, steered across the ice sheet, and found car tracks leading off the lake past the twister-wrecked dance pavilion.

With a flashlight from the glove compartment, I

stepped out into a black wind rattling the boughs overhead. Before me stretched the oak grove, some of its trees felled by the '55 tornado. The snow lay piled in drifts that had just enough crust to make hiking treacherous. One snowbank supported my weight; the next engulfed me hip-deep.

I plodded and waded along, catching shallow breaths of the paralyzingly frigid air.

A cottage loomed ahead—or rather, the remains of one. The twister had lifted away its roof, leaving semi-collapsing walls, from which looters had removed the windows. The snow was heaped through the gaping glassless openings, and above the ruined screen door, the flashlight found painted letters: "Shangri-la."

I trudged on and came upon "Idyllwild." The twister had dropped a tree trunk across its tar-papered roof, and the crash had left no window glass worth stealing.

I hesitated, knifed through by the wind. After all, one Canadian Jones did not make me a man-hunter, and I had no ambition to single-handedly solve this case. It was Willie Popke's job to run down and question the witnesses. But I could not overtake Willie short of Milquevais, and he would have to turn around and drive all the way back to Oak Lake. And then suppose he found no occupied cottage?

I did not want to subject the sheriff to a fifty-mile round trip to discover what I could learn by trudging another fifty yards.

So I reached "Valhalla."

"Valhalla" was a whole cottage, with boarded-up windows from which escaped some chinks of electric illumination. I played the flashbeam upon the snow. Footprints led to the front door, and from the door along the building to the bottled-gas tank and the fuse box and back again.

I approached the door and knocked.

There ensued a brief hush. The wind pincered my cheeks and flowed in chilling trickles up my sleeve ends.

"Hullo in there?" I called.

A feminine voice made up of flute notes answered, "Wait—just a minute—"

I waited, shuffling my feet and breathing into the palm of a glove cupped to shelter my face.

Footfalls tiptoed, a floorboard creaked like a .22 rifle shot, and a key clicked in unoiled door hardware.

The door opened, and I bolted inside with a push from the wind, which reached past me to a pink-shaded drop-cord bulb dangling from the ceiling and started it swaying.

A girl threw her mink-swathed shape against the door. She got it closed, and with a black-gloved hand fought to twist the long-shanked key in the lock.

The room seemed to pitch and sway with the drop bulb's continuing motion. The bulb shed a wan light, dimmed by dust on the globe and tatters of cobweb on the shade.

Against the far wall simmered the twin burners of a gas-fueled stove. It had not been lighted long enough to melt the snow scatters tracked over the bare pine-board floor.

There were also wall shelves, a washstand, an oil-cloth-covered table, chairs, and a daybed, on which were dropped an alligator handbag and a head scarf. The daybed stood against a dry-board partition that made "Valhalla" into two rooms, connected by a curtained doorway. The ceiling was of similar dry board. The other walls showed their two-by-four ribs.

My gaze returned to the girl. Her gaze had been on me all the time.

"Who on earth are you?" she said. Her voice had dropped from the upper-register flute notes.

"The name's Svederup."

The name Svederup appears regularly on by-lined *Globe* stories, but it meant nothing to this young woman. She did not hail from Milquevais—that I knew from the first glance. We have in Milquevais only a small brigade of young women able to afford wild mink coats, and these women do not wear mink while paying visits to dirty, dusty, boarded-up-for-the-winter lake cottages.

Matching the coat was a mink turban, perched on a swirled coiffure of hair as red as an autumn maple leaf. The eye makeup endeavored to make green pupils of hazel ones. The mouth was passion's own wound, but in very cold weather Kelly, too, paints on too much lipstick on the theory it prevents chapping.

"Well?" said the redhead. "What do you want?"

"I saw your light, and I wondered what was up."

"Oh." The green-shadowed eyes looked past me noncommittally.

"What is?" said I.

"What is what?"

"What is up?"

Her expression became that of a housewife about to give the brushoff to the brush salesman.

"You have a nerve barging in here with questions like that," she said.

"I guess I have at that." It was one guess, but for another, the mink coat and the alligator handbag belonged to one world and "Valhalla" to another. So I said, "Still, it's possible you just barged in here, too. A little ahead of me, but being here first doesn't give you any more legal right—"

"That's silly."

"It could be, but you'll have to prove it to me."

"Don't think I can't, only I'm not interested in discussing my personal affairs with you."

"A burglar can't enter a plea of personal affairs to a charge of breaking and entering."

"Breaking and—! You don't suppose I came here to steal the tin cups and the enamel coffeepot?" She laughed. It was a laugh as put-on as her lipstick, and like the lipstick, it was too thick. It decided me.

"I don't know what you're doing here, but I can tell you how I happened to see your light," I said.

She listened to my account of the seining of the ponytailed blonde's body from the lake. Almost at once her head began shaking, and pretty soon she broke in: "But I don't know anything about all that.

How could I? You say this girl, whoever she was, has been dead two or three weeks. It happens I haven't been anywhere near Oak Lake in over six months."

The redhead bent over the daybed, fumbled in the handbag, and found Kents and a lighter. The lighter looked expensive and worked the first time.

She said, "A friend of mine rents this cottage. You can't have me arrested for dropping into a friend's cottage." She began walking about the room. She was wearing plastic protective footgear, translucent enough to reveal high-heeled alligator shoes matching the handbag. "Also, for your information, my husband happens to be an important executive in a big Minneapolis company, and in fact his mother practically owns the company. So don't think I'm a nobody you can push around."

I said, "I don't think you're a nobody. You're somebody, but who? You haven't named your friend or told me your name or made one single statement that can be checked up on."

"Who I am is my business."

"I'm afraid it's the sheriff's and the county attorney's business."

She stopped at the washstand and used the soap dish there as an ash tray.

"My God!" she said. "I haven't got anything to hide. I just don't want to be embarrassed, that's all."

"About what?"

"It's too embarrassing to discuss with you. So can't you just take my word for it and skip the details?"

"No," I said, "but I could do this. I could go to
the courthouse, find in the tax books who owns this
cottage, and from the owner get your friend's name
and from the friend—"

"Oh, all right! My friend is Eva Shelton. And I'm
Midge Holadare—Mrs. James Holadare. And I guess
I might as well tell you the rest of it."

She paused, waiting for an inspiration or something. A boarded-up window above the washstand
made a mirror reflecting our faces.

"I lost my diamond engagement ring up here last
Fourth of July," Midge Holadare said after the
pause. "At that time, I wasn't married to Jim. We
had planned the wedding for June, but his mother
took sick. We were thinking of getting married the
Fourth and going to the Black Hills for a honeymoon,
but Mother Holadare had to see a specialist in New
York, and she took Jim with her. The truth was, she
didn't want him to marry a mere working girl from
the plant and was doing her damnedest to talk Jim
into changing his mind."

"So there I was stuck in Minneapolis over the
Fourth. Well, my friend Eva had this cottage for the
week ends. She invited me to drive up to the lake
with her, and I did. Some friends of Eva's stopped
in. It was a hot night, and we got to drinking Bloody
Mary's and beer. And around midnight one of the
men said let's go for a swim. In the nude. As I said,
we had been drinking, and I didn't want to be a
prude. Well, I went in with the rest. We swam out
to a raft in the lake. There were girls hanging onto

the raft and the fellows pulling them off and ducking them." She stared at me. "You ever notice," she said, "how a person only has to step out of line a little bit and Fate is right there to lower the boom?"

I thought of Kelly in the Tijuana jail. "Sometimes it looks that way."

"The next morning my diamond was gone, and I thought I must have worn it in swimming and lost it out around the raft. You understand, I could hardly tell Jim how I lost his ring. It would just have gone to prove his mother was probably right about me."

The wind went on making eerie music. Drafts seeped into the cottage and swirled around my ankles. The curtain dangling in the partition doorway twitched and rippled.

"Eva is a part-time model," Midge Holadare said. "She does some posing for an artist by the name of Dirk Lebijohn. Lebijohn makes a hobby of hypnotism."

Her voice was again up at the flute end of the scale. Her eyes peeped out of the glades of green eye shadow. The impression came to me of wildlife lurking in a thicket, warily.

"They say people in a trance can remember things from their subconscious," she went on, "and to make a long story short, I let Lebijohn hypnotize me, and I did remember taking off the ring that night and putting it on the stand here."

At the redhead's side, I gazed down at the washstand—a piece of farmhouse furniture covered with oilcloth and shoved up to a close fit between the wall's studding, leaving a finger-breadth crack between it and the cottage siding.

"I bet it fell down behind there," Midge Holadare said. "Only the stand's nailed in place. I've been looking around for a piece of wire, an old coat hanger, so I could try and fish it up."

I tried pulling at the washstand. It was nailed to the two-by-four's, all right. Anything lost behind it six months ago would still be there.

I said, "Well, I happen to have a spud in my car."

Her eyebrows puzzled.

"A spud is a kind of crowbar."

I flashlighted my trip through and over the drifts to the station wagon. From the back end I pulled out the spud and a lap robe. At the side door I reached in for the camera, fed in a fresh filmholder and flashbulb. I wrapped the camera in the robe and carried the bundle under one arm, pointing the flashlight out of that hand and carrying the spud in the other hand. Loaded down with all this weight, I found none of the snowbanks would support me. A country reporter sometimes has to work hard for a couple of inches of news.

FIVE

She had me locked out. There was a delay about letting me in, and when she opened the door, she explained that it had to be locked or the wind would blow it open. In the middle of this chatter, a cannonade thundered in off the lake.

"What—what—?" she half shrieked, on an edge as sharp as a Gillette blade.

"Expanding ice," I said, casually placing the robe-wrapped camera on the table. "As the lake freezes deeper something has to give and the ice cracks up."

She peered doubtfully into the night before slamming and relocking the door.

I slipped the spud's chisel end behind the washstand and made a fulcrum of a two-by-four studding. Rusted nails squeaked, pained pine wood squalled, and after three loosening thrusts I shoved the washstand away from the wall.

There fell to the floor a nest of dust and cobwebs and human hair, toothbrushes and bobby pins and pocket combs, slivers of soap and bits of dental floss —the debris of years composted and honeycombed together.

Midge Holadare went to her knees in a swirl of fur, and her kid-gloved fingers went to crumbling and sorting through the junk. I rested the spud against the wall and slipped my hands into the robe and grasped the Speed Graphic.

The redhead leaped up, exclaiming "Yes, here it is!"

I yanked up the camera, and the flashbulb bathed her in a miniature star-shell explosion.

It left her petrified, staring at me as if I'd turned into the Abominable Snowman.

"—mean by that?" she said, finally finding words.

"Look. I did you a favor, but on my paper's time."

"Paper?" she said as if the Abominable Snowman talked an unknown Himalayan dialect.

"I'm a reporter on the Milquevais *Globe*."

A floorboard squealed as she fled behind the washstand. My eyes glimpsed a movement in the looking-glass window. I turned my head in time to see the partition curtain being swept aside.

A man bulled out of the backroom of "Valhalla" like a figure out of TV Late Show—wearing a trenchcoat and a porkpie hat. His right hand, buried in a slash pocket, raised the coat's skirt. I saw a leg encased in faded blue jeans. I also saw earmuffs flanking the face under the porkpie brim. The face included knobby cheekbones, narrowed eyes, pinched nostrils, and lips thin and blue with cold. He was forty, maybe fifty years of age. He might have been a mobster who had matured into a middle-aged Big House yardbird type.

"Drop the box, Mac, and get 'em up high."

He sounded mean and full of hate. I put down the

camera and raised my hands, not very high, since winter-weight topcoats aren't tailored with much shoulder room.

"Grab your stuff, Midge," the man said.

Her eyes were blanks.

"We're scramming the hell out of here," he said. His free hand stage-directed her. But it was bad stage direction, for Midge Holadare stepped in front of him on her way to the daybed, giving me a chance to grab the spud leaning against the wall.

I slung the five-foot bar at the guy's legs. In the small room it was like shotgunning a fish in a rain barrel.

The spud clipped him below the knee of the nearest leg. He aahhed! through gritted teeth, bending double, clutching at the injured shin.

I jumped in and grabbed his right arm in a hammerlock. His right hand was empty. There was something in the slash pocket. I dug out a roll of fifty-dollar bills, around twenty of them.

He sat down on the daybed to nurse the hurt leg. His hat had fallen off, and the earmuffs bracketed a pompadour of sandy hair that at the nape blossomed into a raggedly scissored ducktail. He now appeared to be neither gangster nor yardbird, but a 1920-vintage beatnik.

He looked up from inspecting a bruised and slightly bloody shin. "Give me back my money," he said.

"Where'd you get it?"

"What's it to you? Maybe I sold a picture."

"I take it you're the artistic Mr. Lebijohn?"

Midge Holadare came between us. "Give him his money." She bent down and picked up the hat and handed it to him. I tossed the roll of fifties into the hat.

He didn't thank me. "Why must you publish Midge's photo in your filthy jerkwater rag?" he asked oratorically and venomously. "I'll tell you why. It's because somebody invented the camera. Press the button and it does the rest. Then they invented robots to press the button. You're a kept press robot, trampling on the individual's right to privacy—"

"Now wait a minute." It wasn't that I cared what he thought; I defended the ethics of journalism for my own benefit. "Losing valuables is a universal human experience," I said. "Recovering the lost article is always good human-interest copy, especially when it's done by means of dreams or fortune-telling or fisherman's luck. And ever since Bridey Murphy, hypnotism has had its own Nielsen rating. The wire services may pick up the story." I grinned at Lebijohn. "You may do a land-office business hypnotizing people who want to find their lost family jewels, mislaid insurance policies, or loaned books."

Midge Holadare caught up her head scarf and pressed it to her mink-clad bosom as if staunching a wound. "You'd be crucifying me!"

"I don't intend to include the midnight swim."

"You'd still be crucifying me."

"Just by printing that you lost your ring, were

hypnotized, and in a trance remembered where you'd put it?"

"Yes. If anything gets in the papers about the ring, I'm sunk."

"Why?"

"You'll have to understand my state of mind last Fourth of July. I loved Jim, but that was the second postponement, and it started to look as if he might be just a mama's boy. I began to realize I'd be making the mistake of my life if I married him, so I decided to break off the engagement unless Jim would break off from her."

"Well?" I said.

"I broke off the engagement, but I couldn't give him back the ring. It was at the bottom of Oak Lake so far as I knew."

I repeated, "Well?"

"You see, I'd told him I must have left the ring in the restroom of the plant and somebody must have picked it up."

"Mrs. Holadare, can't you come to the point?"

"It brought Jim to his senses, and over the Labor Day holiday we got married against his mother's wishes." Her eyes peeped out of the green makeup guiltily. "Now if it comes out the ring was in this cottage all the time, what's Mother Holadare going to make of it? She'll think I not only and in fact hid the ring to avoid having to give it back when I broke the engagement; she'll throw it all in Jim's face and make him eat it. You'll be helping her push me and

Jim into a divorce. And all for a newspaper item people will read one minute and forget the next. Does it mean so much you're willing to smash my life to pieces?"

Midge Holadare tipped up at me a face full of pleading. Then her face seemed to melt and change into Kelly's.

I asked myself how I could go along with keeping the Tijuana arrest out of the *Globe* if I insisted on making news of Midge Holadare's personal affairs. And the idea took another twist: if I gave Midge a break, I could feel better about accepting a break for Kelly and myself. So I said, "You win. I won't make any publicity for you."

There's a nice warm glow that comes of playing God and making people's problems end in happy solutions.

"Then it's a promise? And I can go home to Jim and forget all this ever happened?"

"It's a promise," and in the nice warm glow we exchanged chummy smiles.

"Your car must be nearby," she said, "you weren't gone long. The thing is, I parked out on the highway for fear of getting stuck in here. I don't know how Dirk will make out walking that far, and maybe you could give us a lift to the road?"

I agreed. In a nice warm glow of helpfulness, I shoved the washstand back into its place while she turned off the stove. I gathered up the camera and robe and flashlight while she knotted the scarf under her chin, retrieved the spud while she picked up her handbag. She went ahead to unlock the door.

"Wait a minute," I said. "Where'd you get the key?"

"It's a skeleton—"

"You were here six months ago and you remembered a skeleton key would do the trick?"

"Yes," she said. "All ready. We'll go out first, Dirk, and you can turn out the light."

The light was something else. The customary thing in boarding up a summer cottage is to disconnect the electricity. "And you thought to bring a fuse for the box?" I said.

"No, but Dirk knew where the fuses are kept."

I looked at Lebijohn, waiting under the drop-cord bulb.

"Eva only used the place week ends," Midge Holadare said. "She let Dirk come up for a few days during the summer. He painted some landscapes."

"You mean like Van Gogh?" I said, studying the beatnik.

"No, not like Van Gogh," Lebijohn said, making the name rhyme with 'coke.' "I paint like myself. You wouldn't understand."

"Why don't you two stop spatting?" the red head said. "Let me carry the flashlight."

We made our way to the station wagon, she following in my tracks and Lebijohn limping in hers. I tossed the stuff in the back; we shared the front seat, Midge in the middle; we followed a quarter-mile of snow-choked dirt road out to Highway 12. The headlights showed up some rural mailboxes mounted on wheels on top of posts, and a parked white T-bird.

I braked. Lebijohn got out and stumped away toward the T-bird. Midge Holadare started to get out, but instead pulled shut the Chevie door and twisted to me.

"You've been awfully sweet." Her white breath crossed six inches to reach my face. "I don't think Jim would mind one small and very grateful kiss."

Somewhere in space a satellite traveled a hundred miles while I considered whether to move my mouth the six inches.

"Your Jim may be more broad-minded than my wife," I said finally. But that was not my reason.

The boy scout who's led the old lady across the intersection doesn't like to be tipped a penny for his service, particularly when he needs to chalk up the good deed to square himself with himself. Particularly if he figures the penny is counterfeit.

"I guess you're right, and considering the weather, we ought to settle for rubbing noses like the Eskimos do."

The light touch was counterfeit, too.

She started to open the door again, then turned back again and said, "Oh, we almost forgot. You didn't give me my picture."

So that was what she was after, and she must have hoped a kiss would soften me up.

"I didn't forget," I said. "I'm keeping the film."

"Why? You promised you wouldn't put me in your paper, and now I don't know what to think."

"I could run the story without your picture; most news stories are run that way."

"I know, but—"

"But you could deny the whole thing unless I had your picture as proof?"

"No! It's just that I don't like a total stranger snapping and keeping my picture, and I bet your wife would feel the same way."

The dragging of Kelly into it didn't improve my mood.

"My wife might not like it, but she might have to take her medicine."

"You won't sound so smug about it if the day ever comes." Midge Holadare wrenched open the door and leaped out into the snow and ran to the T-bird. I watched her vanish into it, saw the tailpipes spew fumes, the headlights come on, and the white car turn across the highway, headed for the Cities. I drove the other way, toward Milquevais.

On the way my thoughts pounded like the threshing of the chains on the pavement. I said to myself that Midge Holadare couldn't have dreamed it all up on the spur of the moment and therefore her tale must be more or less true.

But not necessarily the full truth.

Maybe the lost ring had been insured. Maybe she had collected the insurance. Maybe she did not want the insurance company to learn the diamond had been found.

It was even possible that 'way back last July she had deliberately "lost" the ring. If she'd felt the engagement had reached the breaking-off point, losing the engagement diamond would have been an excuse for not giving it back to Jim Holadare.

I could smell more than the reek of the car heater.

Maybe I should have made a citizen's arrest and turned Midge Holadare and Dirk Lebijohn over to the sheriff.

Willie Popke wouldn't have let them off so easily, and for one thing I felt sure Willie would have impounded the diamond ring. When anything as valuable as a diamond or an automobile gets into a sheriff's hands, he can't release it to just anybody who says "It's mine." There'd have to be proof of legal ownership. If Jim Holadare gave it to her, he'd have to come up to Milquevais with a bill of sale from the jeweler to prove his ownership.

If I had it all to do over, what would I have done?

I still hadn't decided when I overtook the Busch Brothers truck creeping around a curve, with the wind bellying the tarpaulin shroud over the unknown's dead and frozen body, and I wondered, "Coincidence?"

I had to admit there didn't have to be a connection between Midge Holadare and the ponytailed blonde.

I passed the roadside sign that announced: ENTERING MILQUEVAIS. Ahead loomed the Farmers Cooperative Creamery, plate glass and glass brick shining in the darkness like an illuminated gigantic ice cube.

A Mud Hen switch engine blocked the end of Main Street with a string of boxcars. I drove down to Superior Street, turned at the Prairie States Fuel & Refrigerants warehouse, and drove crosstown to the courthouse square. In the red-brick jail behind the courthouse a light burned in the sheriff's office. The courthouse loomed as dark as a cemetery monument. I steered from the frozen, deserted street into the alley, and from the alley into the *Globe* parking lot. A bulb over the pressroom door diffused dim rays of light over three or four parked and blanketed cars.

I braked and stepped out into what was now minus twenty-five-degree cold, the kind of cold you taste to the roots of your front teeth. Underfoot lay some slicks of ice where dribbles from parked-car radiators had leaked and frozen.

Through the black, searing cold, skating gingerly on the ice slicks, I moved around to the tail gate.

I wanted the lap robe to throw over the Chevie's nose, and the camera.

I'd just pulled these things out of the station wagon when they fired the courthouse cannon.

That's how it sounded and felt.

The parking lot and everything in it blew up around me in a jarring, blinding flash and roar.

SIX

Inside the pressroom Lem Bergstrom, seated at his linotype keyboard, heard a pounding at the door.

"Yeah, come in."

Lem went on setting up a Personals ad: *Dolly, meet me at the Elite Cafe any nite this week for the biggest burger in town.*

The pounding was not repeated, but not very much later a chilling draft flung Lem around.

"Crysake, shut the door!" he hollered.

"Help—Kenny's hurt—"

And there, supporting and guiding me through the open doorway, was Leslie Jopperman.

I did not know it. I was on my feet, but out on my feet. You will have to take Lem's word for it that my right hand clutched my Speed Graphic.

"Hey? What?" cried Bergstrom.

"I guess poor Kenny slipped on the ice and knocked himself out," said Les.

I came to sitting in Ed Horace's swivel chair, holding the camera in my lap, being interrogated by the managing editor's bifocal-bracketed eyes. I saw his glasses and eyes clearly, but had the impression his ears were made of mist.

"Are you all right, Ken? Do you want me to call a doctor?"

I said I was all right. I was not going to die, but I'd been shaken up and had an actively aching area at the back of my head.

"We ought to throw ashes on them ice puddles— do it before somebody breaks his neck," Lem Bergstrom said.

I had no memory of falling, but it didn't seem important.

"Kenny might have paid with his life if I hadn't come along," said Les Jopperman. "He could have frozen to death without recovering consciousness."

I wondered what Les was doing in Milquevais, but that didn't seem important either.

And now Bergstrom: "Who knocked on the door, though?"

"What do you mean, knocked on the door?" said Ed Horace.

"I mean knocked on the door a minute or so before you came in."

"That's impossible. There was no one in sight except Kenny sprawled on the ground behind his car," said Les Jopperman.

"All the same, somebody knocked."

None of it was important, and then I looked down at the Speed Graphic on my lap and saw that the filmholder was missing. The film had still been in the camera when I walked from "Valhalla" and tossed my stuff into the back of the station wagon.

"Of course, I wasn't looking for loiterers," Les Jopperman said. "I had eyes only for Kenny, actually."

I thought Midge Holadare wanted the film badly enough to bop me, and no doubt Lebijohn would have done it for her. But the white T-bird had not overtaken me on the road. They could only have done it by taking a country road to Wydota, then traveling over Highway 8. But how could they have known that the place to lie in wait was the parking lot behind the *Globe* building?

"Have you got your wallet all right, Kenny?"

I unbuttoned the topcoat and felt and said, "Yes, it's here."

"It's possible my arrival frightened off an assailant who was after the wallet, though."

"Why would a thief after the wallet knock on the door before stealing the wallet?" Ed Horace said.

"I don't know," said Les. "I'm game to go out there and look around."

"I'll go with you," and Bergstrom followed Jopperman out of the office. Ed Horace closed the door and returned and stood studying me. He was now sucking throughtfully on his unlighted pipe.

My feeling about it ran that somebody lurking among the parked cars had felled me with a blow from behind, had snatched the holder from the camera, and had fled after knocking on the door. I did not see how Midge could have moved fast enough, and yet if I told the truth about the episode, I would have to tell what was on the stolen film. I would have to name her after promising not to, and she might not be responsible for the slugging.

"You sure you're okay?" Ed asked.

I said I was okay, and it was true—I now saw his ears clearly.

He sighed. "I'm sorry, but I'm afraid it's bad news."

The words woke me up like a cold shower. "You called the consul?"

"Yes, and he can't do much—this raid was a big deal and full of politics. They have forty-five to fifty Americans in the jug, and they mean to play it tough and make an example of them."

"What the hell?"

"Big-time gamblers have been trying to move in, and this is the crackdown."

"Kelly isn't a big-time gambler."

Ed played the pipestem across his teeth. "It's their law. Their law makes patronizing a gaming establishment just as bad a crime as operating one."

"She wasn't even patronizing. Just a tourist looking on."

"In their books, being a spectator is punished by the same dose."

"Well, my *God!*"

"The dose can be a fine of four hundred dollars and anything up to three years in the penitentiary."

"Crazy," I said.

"I know, but the consul can't do anything, and can't advise anything except be ready with the bail, and it will be pretty stiff bail when they get around to setting it. He expects the same as the fine, four hundred dollars, because these American citizens naturally won't remain in Mexico awaiting trial."

Kelly and I had a very little over nine hundred dollars in the joint checking account, so I thought about the four hundred. But I didn't think about it very long.

I said, "What's he mean, when they get around to setting it?"

"Under their law, when the judge gets damned good and ready to hear the case. That's the preliminary hearing. The trial itself might be a year off. And if the bail isn't forthcoming the prisoner goes to the penitentiary for the year or however long it takes."

"Hit me again, I'm still breathing."

"I hate to, Ken, but you'd better airmail your mother-in-law a certified check first thing in the morning. Be ready with the bail. Your wife's locked up in an eight-by-ten cell with seven other women."

Time is relative. A few eons of it wheeled around my head. Space is relative. Across a few galaxies of it came the sound of knuckles drumming on the office door.

Ed lifted his head and raised his voice. "Wait a minute out there." He bent his face close to mine and lowered his voice. "Some of these details I got from the news-ticker. Close to half a hundred U.S. citizens getting this kind of a deal, well, it's building up into an international incident."

From ranging in time and space, my thoughts came home to roost. They were personal thoughts, unconcerned with the Oak Lake ponytailed blonde or the redhead with the lost diamond or the beatnik painter making a sideline of hypnotism.

"If Kelly's mixed up in an international incident, the *Globe* can't soft-pedal the story," I said.

"I leave that up to you, Ken."

"I say print the facts." The decision came unheroically. A few lines of type no longer seemed important. "Eight by ten is barely bigger than a bathroom," I said.

"Don't make things worse than they are." Ed crossed the office and opened the door to Les Jopperman. Les bustled in, his kewpie countenance glowing with cold and excitement. He brought with him and placed on the littered desk my camera case.

"There are no signs of robbery, would you say, Kenny?"

I lifted the case's saddle leather lid and peered in. It contained a carton of photo bulbs, a lens shade and assorted filters, a light meter, and a stack of film-holders. After shooting a picture a photographer reverses the holder slides, and by the reversed slides I identified the holder containing the shots of the fishing crew and of Bowers showing Popke and Doc Soole the hole in the ice.

The whole Oak Lake incident seemed long gone and faraway. The fact that only the "Valhalla" film was missing impressed me about as much as a mosquito in the bedroom bothers a man who wakes up and hears a burglar in the house.

"It works out to eighty square feet divided by eight is barely a square yard per person," I said.

"I don't get you, Kenny," said Les, rolling his eyes.

I spoke to Ed Horace. "The hell with airmailing a check. I'll fly out to the West Coast myself." The thought was sheer inspiration, undreamed of a moment earlier.

"What good can you do?" Ed said.

"There must be some way of cutting the red tape, and at least I'm an able-bodied man, and Kelly's mother is in a wheel chair. If nothing else, Kelly will feel better knowing I'm there to take the worry off her mother's shoulders."

The pipestem played *tic-tac-toe* over Ed Horace's teeth.

"It's a little like a funeral in the family," I said. "Maybe my being there won't change anything, but I feel I should go."

Ed looked badgered, his eyes more than usually schizophrenic, the double personalities of human being and managing editor debating.

"I don't know if I can let you go. It's leaving the paper shorthanded, and with a big story breaking."

He had a point. All Crossway papers are short-handed as a matter of policy, and the *Globe*'s small staff included nobody with the spare time to cover my beat.

I had another inspiration. I said, "There's Jopperman here. He could sub for me."

I looked at Les in time to see his kewpie face flood full of lovely, agreeable, cooperative eagerness.

"Jopperman already has a job," Ed said.

"He doesn't work twenty-four hours a day at it. He was at the lake today, and he's here now. There's the five o'clock southbound, and then not another train until around ten, isn't it?"

"Ten-o-two, the local," said Les.

"That's five hours, and he could do most of the leg-work simply by phoning the sheriff and the county attorney. He could have the story whipped in shape by eight o'clock at night, and either bring it in or hire some Wydota high school kid to bring it in."

"The story, yes," said Ed. "But this arrangement leaves the paper without any camera coverage."

I did a quick-think.

"Look, Ed, I'm sure I can chase around tonight and scare up some pictures, leave you a supply you can feed into the paper from day to day."

"I never heard of such a thing." Ed looked un-easily at the wall. "What would the Old Man say?"

"He'll never know the difference, and I'll prove it to you. Les can sit right down to a typewriter and start batting out the story, and I'll rush out and grab the pix. Prove it to you, Ed."

"You can try to prove it to me."

SEVEN

It had gotten colder outside. The tire chains rang almost like sleighbells on the frozen pavement leading to the Milquevais Public Library. The reading-room windows were darkened, but a light glowed in Miss Florrie Schultz's office.

I knocked at the library's side door and did an Indian war dance until Miss Florrie Schultz let me into the steam-heated, book-scented building.

"Why, Kenneth, whatever—?"

"Miss Schultz, I realize this sounds funny, but could you lend me your bathing suit?"

Florrie Schultz regarded me through splendid intellectual eyes that did research for me and corrected the chapters of my novel for errors in spelling and punctuation. I had often wondered whether Miss Schultz, after hours in the library, was secretly writing a novel of her own. But there was nothing on her desk except a stack of overdue book notices she'd been running through the typewriter.

"What an extraordinary request, Kenneth. I don't have one here. You'll have to drive me home."

Florrie has never learned to drive a car and hikes everywhere in defiance of the worst weather.

She opened a closet door and began garbing herself in a common-sense hiking attire of overshoes and stout cloth cloak and stocking cap. I looked down at the overdue cards on the desk.

"You don't happen to be missing any blonde pony-tailed patrons lately, do you, Miss Schultz?"

"I think not, Kenneth. Why?"

I told Florrie about the Oak Lake victim while she hooded the typewriter, and we left by and locked the side door and headed the station wagon toward her duplex apartment.

"It seems to me, Miss Schultz, that any young woman who could have disappeared two or three weeks ago may have lived a lonely life, and lonely people are frequently great readers, and you might have known her."

Florrie's splendid intellectual eyes stared straight ahead through the windshield. She inquired, "How is the novel progressing, Kenneth?"

"Slowly—"

"Perhaps it would progress faster if you spent more time on it and less time on identifying bodies for Sheriff Popke. You were going to get so much done while Kelly's away."

"Speaking of Kelly—" and I spoke of Kelly during the rest of the trip and while we left the Chevie and climbed the stairs to the duplex.

Miss Schultz was disturbed by the story.

"It's dreadful, and naturally you're shocked for your wife's sake, but I hope the *Globe* won't play up the injustice to *her*. I'm sure when you get there you'll find more Mexicans than Americans in the jail. It's the unfortunate Mexican people who suffer the most from living under such medieval laws, and we should sympathize, instead of hating them as a people."

"The bathing suit, Miss Schultz."

Leaving me in the living room—a place about as homey as the library's reading room—Florrie retired to her bedroom and presently returned with a swim-suit—a one-piece garment made of Lastex-like material having a white background overlaid with large, stylized, Hawaiian-like flowers done in blue.

"Where'd you get this, Miss Schultz?"

"At the Crane Store's Harvest Days sale. They had a tableful of them marked down from $17.50 to $4.95, I think it was."

"All blue-on-white ones?"

"I think so. That would explain the price: most women want to look a little different from the next one—although they haven't any objection to thinking all alike."

In the black-shadowed Ford garage shop, a mechanic was cautiously weaving a blowtorch under the Busch Brothers' truck bed. Supervising the job stood our county attorney, Walter Burch.

Burch was a square-chinned, clear-eyed, grass-roots politician—a grass-roots politician being a public officeholder too smart to be caught photographed pitching hay (the farmers use hayloaders nowadays), but willing to pose on a tractor seat.

Walter Burch was also willing to pose with the Busch brothers, studying some mysterious papers (they came off the shop foreman's hook), and examining an ice spud such as might have been used to bury the victim (my own spud). Then I snapped him looking for clues in Miss Florrie Schultz's swimsuit.

The swimsuit interested him. He got on the phone to call Henry Crane about the Harvest Days sale, and I snapped a final photo of him using the phone.

I didn't tell Burch why I needed so many pictures, even though he would read of Kelly's arrest in the morning *Globe*. He would have wanted to wire the congressman, and a newspaperman can't afford to be indebted to a politician for favors. Besides, I figured the Congressman would only pass the buck to the State Department.

I needed money for the trip—bail money, plane fare both ways, incidentals, maybe a fee to hire a Tijuana lawyer who'd know the ins and outs of Mexican law. It meant cleaning out the bank account, but I hoped to be on the plane by the time the bank opened in the morning, and I wanted to avoid the delay of visiting gas stations and drugstores and poolhalls picking up fifty dollars from one cash register and a hundred from the next.

So after Walter Burch finished phoning, I rang up old Olin Wolff, the treasurer of the Farmers Cooperative Creamery. Could the Co-op cash my personal check for nine hundred dollars?

"Why, sure, young fellow. Glad to oblige."

"Fine, Mr. Wolff. Suppose I drive by the house and pick you up?"

"You don't have to. Swedenborg and I are going down to the office and work on the annual report, anyway." Swedenborg was his son and the assistant treasurer (Mrs. Wolff had been a religious mystic). "You get there first, pound on the door, and Jessie will let you in." Jessie was Jessica Riker, Ralph Riker's wife.

Back at the *Globe* office, Leo Spenser took the films down to his basement developing and engraving lab. At my desk in the newsroom, Leslie Jopperman sat alternately ceiling-gazing for inspiration and then whacking a machine-gun staccato on the typewriter.

"How are you doing, Les?" I asked.

"Well, I think at last I've managed to hit the right notes of mystery and menace—"

I bent over to skim the copy sheafing from the platen.

It was uncanny. In his first twenty-five words he'd managed to invoke the Oak Lake silences and to paint the scene, and infuse it with suggestions of dread and eerie doom.

"Swell!" I said. "Only you first have to strike the notes of who, when, and where. You begin with Sheriff William Popke instead of just the anonymous "local authorities." The dead woman is a dead woman and not a Murdered Milquevais Mermaid. And you don't have to suggest that the lakes around here may all be full of female corpses."

The kewpie face clouded sourly. "Why does it have to be so cut and dried? You don't have the im-

agination to comprehend my method, so let me explain—"

"Hold on, Les. I don't have the imagination to
comprehend what you were doing in the parking lot
a while ago, either. If you want to explain something, you can start with that."

The grimace became a sickly grin. "Well, Kenny,
sure I can explain. I had an idea I wanted to take up
with you, but it was just an idea and doesn't seem so
important any more."

"Yes, and you've got an idea here—an emotional
impression instead of the cut-and-dried facts. The
trouble is, Ed Horace will blue-pencil all the fancy
atmospheric writing, and there won't be any story
left. He's going to balk at letting me go, and I can't
have that. So, here, I'll knock out the lead para-
graph and show you how—"

I drove out to the house to pack a suitcase. Milquevais is a town of home-owners, a fact that makes
it a little tough for young couples looking for a place
to rent. Kelly and I had inspected the available du-
plexes and the few apartments on the upper floors of
the business buildings, and our choice fell on an 1890-
model frame dwelling that had been divided into
flats. We'd leased the downstairs flat, with the backyard garden thrown in; we'd modernized it by painting the floors and mopboards a vivid pink; and we'd
splurged on some $3.45-the-single-roll wallpaper.
Like most old houses, it was short of closet space. I
had to go down in the basement to hunt up a suitcase,

then had to wipe the coal dust off it after I found one. Luckily, the tenants upstairs would keep the furnace going, or I would have had to drain the water pipes before daring to leave the place.

Packing the suitcase took a quarter-hour, and another ten minutes brought me to the Co-op's glass-slab doors. The place was locked. I knocked and rattled the doors. At the top of a flight of steps inside the glass slabs appeared Cuban-heeled pumps and a pair of plump, Turkish-delight calves. Jessica Riker descended the steps. She had thick, peasant thighs encased in a tight black skirt, a strong and big-breasted torso garbed in a silky red blouse. A shawl hid her shoulders, and a fortress of combs guarded the high-piled black hair.

"My, isn't the weather a fright!" Mrs. Riker said. "Your wife's a lucky woman to be in California, and that's for sure. I bet it never snows out there, does it?"

Mrs. Riker's dark complexion and flashing eyes suggested Gypsy ancestry. In fact, her father had been a local well-digger. Jessica had gone to Milquevais high school and to Mankato business college and after working a while in St. Paul had returned to the home town with a husband in tow. Like everyone else, she was going to read in the morning of Kelly's arrest, but I found myself replying, "The weather's in the seventies. They're picking tangerines off the backyard tree."

"Tangerines!" said Mrs. Riker. "Do you realize oranges are forty-three cents the pound at the IGA?

I tell Ralph the frozen juice is just as good and so much cheaper, but no, he has to have his fresh fruit. Nothing but the best for him when it comes to setting the table."

We climbed the stairs and walked along a cork-floored corridor into the treasurer's office. It was a large room made bright by banks of fluorescent lights burning in an electronic-brained bookkeeping machine. We'd had a writeup in the *Globe* when the Co-op installed the machine a couple of years ago. The operator fed punched-holed cards into one end, and out of the other end came the farmers' milk checks.

Mrs. Riker began stuffing the cards into the electronic gullet. "Excuse me for working while we talk but everything's so far behind. You know, Olin Wolff is getting on. He spends most of the time chinning with the farmers and cussing out Ezra Taft Benson. It leaves the whole work load to Swede and me—that's why the overtime."

I wondered why she told me.

"The people don't appreciate Swede. He's so quiet and modest and never lets on actually he's holding down his job and the old man's, too. He hasn't took a vacation in three years, that shows you."

Possibly she thought I was paying a social call and it was her duty to entertain me until the Wolffs arrived.

"I certainly hope when Olin comes to retire the members will see fit to elect Swede to the job," she rattled on. "But you know how the Co-op is—every farmer has the same vote, and most of them don't bother to even read the annual report. The election of officers is just a popularity contest, and Swede is too busy and serious-minded to do the kidding and the handshaking. I tell Ralph the truck drivers ought to get together and put in the good word for Swede amongst the farmers."

The Wolffs arrived.

Olin Wolff was a big, elderly Dane with a thick mane of white hair, shaggy white eyebrows, and a luxuriant white mustache. Swedenborg Wolff was a big, younger Dane with a thick mane of yellow hair, shaggy yellow eyebrows, and a luxuriant yellow mustache.

Olin Wolff looked a bit like La Follette, the old-time Wisconsin senator, a bit like Paul Bunyan; and quite a lot like Santa Claus. Swede only managed to look like a yellow crayon copy of his father.

"Open up the vault, Swede," the old man said. "Come on in and sit down, Sverderup."

The treasurer's private office was a frosted glass enclosure at the side of the big room. Olin Wolff hung up his hat and winter coat, sat down behind his limed-oak desk, and said, "Have a smoke?"

I declined.

He fumbled and took a cigar from a box on the desk, fumbled and found a packet of matches. He lighted up, blew out the match, and dropped it into a tray of metal paper clips on the desk.

"I hope you ain't buying any wildcat oil leases," he said. "I hear a dentist up in Goodlands took three thousand out of the bank and gave it to some wildcat oil promoters the other day."

"It'll all be in the paper in the morning," I began.

Olin Wolff listened and shook his white-maned head. "The world has come to a hell of a pass," he said. "I can remember when the Mexicans pulled the same stunt in Wilson's day, they stuck a couple of U.S. sailors in the hoosegow. And by God, Wilson ordered the Navy to occupy Vera Cruz, and he made the Mexican president salute the United States flag."

"Times change, Mr. Wolff," and according to what I'd heard, in his youth Olin Wolff had been a Non-Partisan League organizer who'd either been sent to jail or threatened with jail for advocating resistance to the World War I draft.

"The government spends all these billions for defense and foreign aid," he was saying, "and then an American citizen has to go and ransom his wife out of jail."

Swede Wolff came in with a cashbox, put it on the desk, and switched up the desk light. "You'll have to take it in twenties, maybe a few tens," he said. He counted out the nine hundred. I opened my checkbook.

"Make it payable to the Co-op?" I asked Olin Wolff.

"Make it out to me," Swede said. "I have to go to the bank in the morning, anyway. I'll cash the check and put the money back in the box and save bookkeeping."

"If I was President, I'd march the Marines into

Tijuana," Olin Wolff said, angrily knocking cigar ash into the tray of paper clips.

I stood up to go.

"Mrs. Riker will let you out," Swede said.

Mrs. Riker and I walked down the cork-floored corridor.

"By the way, I ran into Ralph out in Wydota today," I said. "He was in the railroad station with some kind of shipment."

"Furs, I guess," said Jessica Riker.

"Furs?"

"Yes. You know, a lot of the farm kids set traps and catch a few muskrats, maybe a mink or a fox. Ralph has been buying the furs—it's mostly an accommodation, but it helps make ends meet, too."

We went down the steps. Mrs. Riker hesitated with the door key poised. "The thing is, even if the farmers don't read the annual reports, they do read the *Globe,*" she said. "You know the old saying, one hand washes the other. Any favorable mention of Swede in the paper would be a help and appreciated."

I began to realize I need not have worried about what Jessica Riker or anybody else would think of Kelly's being arrested. They were going to go on thinking as they always thought, and mostly about their own troubles.

It was just as true of me. I slid behind the wheel of the Chevie and headed along Highway 12, toward the Minneapolis airport. The least of my worries was the Murdered Milquevais Mermaid.

EIGHT

The plane banked down from a blue, cloudless California sky, skimmed across a high steel fence, and leveled out on the tar-black of Lindbergh Field. It slowed and turned and taxied back, and the passengers single-filed into the half-shabby, half-bright San Diego scene.

Just inside the gate I was stopped by a hatless, sunburnt man in blue gabardines and a brown-dotted bow tie.

"You must be Svederup. I'm Webb Wilson. Kelly's mother said you wired you were coming, and I promised to meet you." He walked at my side into the airport office. "They'll be a while with the baggage. Let me buy you a coffee and give you a fill-in on the situation," he suggested.

We sat at the counter facing coffees and bear paws.

"I hope you're not blaming Roy Elling," Wilson said earnestly. "He's my wife's kid brother, just a few months out of the service. He'd only been working long enough to save up the down payment on a last year's Dodge. He had no way of knowing the Rosarita Beach club wasn't perfectly legitimate. It'd been running wide open for close to half a year. It had a Federal cop on duty outside the door, and a Tijuana city cop on duty inside, and some kind of a license or permit framed on the wall. Well, Roy and Kelly had just barely walked in when the joint was hit by a squad of Federal plain-clothes dicks waving sawed-off shotguns, lining the customers up and stripping them of their wallets, tossing the money into a gunnysack. The whole thing was pulled off like a stickup, and that's what Roy thought it was. He lost around thirty dollars that he'll never see again. They confiscate the money of anybody nabbed in a gambling raid. They impounded Roy's car, and maybe they'll confiscate that, too, and he may never see it again."

All this sounded almost as if Wilson expected me to chip in and help make up Elling's losses. Instead, he dug into the blue gabardines and laid a key on the counter.

"You're going to need transportation to Tijuana, and I want you to have the use of my Renault. There's just one thing about it. You'll find yourself in a foreign country, up against a lot of tough cops who'll fob you off on the district attorney, and the district attorney will say it's up to the judge, and the judge can't be reached. Don't let it rile you. Don't try throwing your weight around, and don't try throwing money around in a way that could be construed as offering a bribe. And above all, for God's sake, don't take a poke at anybody. Or they'll throw *you* in the calaboose, and probably they'll impound my car."

"I've always been a peaceable and law-abiding citizen, Mr. Wilson. I didn't fly out here with the idea of engineering a jailbreak."

"You flew out here with the idea of pulling off something," Wilson said.

I denied it.

"You're figuring on cutting a corner somewhere," Wilson said. "I took a half-day off Monday, and it was all I could do to deliver some blankets to the jail for Kelly and Roy."

Tijuana was a duty bordertown with a couple of garish thoroughfares featuring bazaars and import shops and cantinas, backed up by smaller streets lined with buildings that gave the impression of being built of packing boxes and soft-drink signboards. The jail was built of gritty concrete, enclosed along with a few dried-up trees in a dusty yard.

The guard at the gate had an answer to everything. The answer was No *sabe, senor*."

So I drove the Renault around awhile and found the office of A. Gaitterez, lawyer.

Senor Gaitterez was a big, corpulent man of about Webb Wilson's sunburnt complexion, and of about Wilson's pessimistic temperament.

"It concerns my wife," I began.

"You wish to arrange the divorce?"

"I wish to arrange to get her out of jail."

"The divorce would be easier," said Senor Gaitterez.

"At least, I want to get in and see her."

"It is not permitted that relatives visit the prisoners."

"She must be entitled to legal counsel?" said I. "Maybe you can get me in there?"

Senor Gaitterez put on a large pair of butterfly-wing sunglasses and accompanied me to the jail. He got me in—I did not realize at the time what a feat that was.

The jail was as filthy as the inside of a slop bucket, and smelled like the inside of a slop bucket. It was cold, too. The guard inside was hunched into a leather jacket to keep warm.

The guard, Senor Gaitterez, and I climbed to the second floor, where an open skylight over the corridor let in the cold without letting out any of the smell. We stopped in front of a grated door. I peered through the grating, and made out the figures of the eight female prisoners, some standing and some seated, and all huddled into the folds of improvised blanket ponchos. There were benches or bare wooden bunks ranged around the walls.

"Kelly!" I called.

One of the blanket-draped shapes turned around and squeezed through the other shapes to reach the grating.

Kelly is a toast brown brunette, and the girl in the cell had neatly combed toast brown hair. The girl in the cell had Kelly's cute features, and she'd managed to wash the face and apply the lipstick. But somehow or other, she didn't look like the Kelly I was used to facing across the breakfast table back in Milquevais. She looked more as if Kelly had died and turned into a zombie.

"Ken!" Her voice didn't sound like Kelly's voice, either. "Where'd you come from?"

"Your mother called—I flew out— Hey, stop crying!"

"I'm not crying—sneedzing. I caught such a hell of a cold the first night in here—"

I whipped out a handkerchief and succeeded in stuffing it through the grating before the guard grabbed my arm. He yelled something in my face, a mixture of Spanish and foul breath. I looked at Senor Gaitterez.

"Passing articles to the prisoner is not permitted," Senor Gaitterez translated.

"But she's sick." I peered in at Kelly. "You're sick. You need a doctor."

"It's only a head cold," Kelly said.

"Can't you arrange for a doctor to give her a shot?" I said to Senor Gaitterez.

"I don't want one of their doctors sticking a needle into me," Kelly said.

"An American doctor, then."

"They wouldn't let an American practice medicine across the line," said Kelly.

The guard said something in Spanish.

"It is not permitted to insult the national culture and institutions," Senor Gaitterez translated.

"If he sabies English, why don't he talk English?" I said.

The guard talked English. "The time is up, and now you vamose."

"We haven't had a chance to say anything yet," I said.

The guard pulled at my arm. I felt like slugging him.

"Good-bye, Ken," said Kelly.

"I'll get you some aspirin and some paper hankies and—"

"Vamose!"

"See you tomorrow if you're not out of here befor then!"

"And, Ken, tell mother I'm all right—don't mention the sniffles—"

Senor Gaitterez and I returned to the street. He inserted his bulk beside me in the small car. My fingers shook, trying to stab the key into the ignition lock.

"Penal conditions are not invariably admirable in the States," the lawyer said. "There are overcrowded prisons—chain gangs—insane asylums where the patients are kicked and beaten."

"Look! There must be some way of getting my wife out of that hell hole!"

"The law can only move with all deliberate speed."

"How about a writ of habeas corpus?" I suggested.

"Our Mexican law is based upon the Napoleonic Code. Permit me to explain the Code—"

He was still explaining it when I dropped him at his office.

I drove to the shopping section, bought aspirin and cold tablets and nose drops and a basket of fruit, and then brought them back and left them with the gate sentry.

At the U.S. consulate, I found several dozen friends and relatives of the jailed Americans listening to an explanation of the Napoleonic Code. As far as I could make out, the Napoleonic Code works like the steel traps in the muskrat houses back home. Once the trap springs on the muskrat's foot, the muskrat can escape only by chewing the foot off.

At the International gate, a U.S. Immigration man wanted to know where I was born, and a Customs man wanted to know what I'd bought in Mexico.

That was the first day.

The days passed. I stayed with Kelly's mother in La Jolla. La Jolla is a seaside suburb that begins with surf pounding on the sea cliffs and creaming upon the beaches. It is a town of old redwood cottages built during the eighties and nineties, stucco and red-tile-roofed homes of the First World War era, frowning mansions left when the 1929 bubble burst, modern-day middle-class ranchhouses costing as much as the 1929 mansions did, and hilltop estates worth the price of a seat on the New York Stock Exchange. It is also a town of chainstores and giftshops and tennis courts and swimming pools, all stitched together with palm trees and eucalyptus and bougainvillea under a sky shaken by the thunder and sonic booms of jet planes.

Kelly's father had died in 1943, leaving Kelly's

mother a partly paid-for bungalow in the old part of
town near the high school and a fixed annuity income
that had been modest in 1943. With Kelly in jail,
Mrs. Kelly had been compelled to install a practical
nurse in the spare bedroom.

So I had Kelly's room. I hung my things from my
suitcase in the closet along with her dresses and
stowed my shirts in the same drawer with her
lingerie.

I woke up mornings, got through with the bathroom ahead of the practical, put on the coffeepot,
gathered a handful of tangerines from the tree, and
brought in the San Diego morning paper from the
front porch.

At breakfast I studied the continuing front-page
Tijuana serial. It remained fundamentally the same
story. One day local public officials called for Con-
gressional action to close the border to keep U.S.
tourists from spending money in the Mexican stores;
the next day, several congressmen called the situation
to the attention of the U.S. State Department; the
day after that, the State Department notified the congressmen that the problem was being taken under
advisement. Meanwhile, the Americans stayed in jail.

Shortly after nine o'clock every morning, the post-
man left the mail, which included an airmailed copy
of the previous day's Milquevais *Globe*. The first was
headlined:

OAK LAKE GIRL A GAS VICTIM. Coroner Soole
had found post-mortem indications of carbon monoxide poisoning, possibly the result of inhaling auto-

mobile exhaust fumes. The further indications were that the victim had been a young woman of between twenty-five and thirty years of age, five feet, four and a half in height, weighing one-twenty pounds, who had, shortly before her death, consumed one and a half ounces of bread and a small tumberful of choco-late-flavored skim milk.

So far, Ed Horace had heavily blue-penciled Les-lie Jopperman's prose, but as I read on, the evidences of Les's talent thickened. Les pointed out that the bread and milk might have been a bedtime snack, that the ventilation holes to be found in most storm sash were of exactly the size to receive the nozzle of a hose, that there might be in Milquevais County a maniac who went around squirting poison fumes into the bedchambers of sleeping young women.

Swimsuit Traced to Milquevais Store. The swimsuit was a product of Glover-Gleason, a Chicago manufacturer. It had been made to be fair-traded at $17.75 retail price, under the firm's Gee-Gee Beach-wear label. There'd been a season-end surplus, so they'd removed the labels and job-lotted the suits, and Henry Crane of the Crane Department Store had made a special purchase of five dozen to be fea-tured as a $4.98 Harvest Days special. About half of these garments had been sold to customers with charge accounts, and Henry Crane had furnished County Attorney Burch with a list of their names. The trouble was that other suits had been sold for cash, and one of the Crane store salesgirls remembered a bearded man paying cash for four of the swimsuits. He had acted "nervous and funny."

Les Jopperman took it from there, went on to suggest that the bearded man might be a demented killer who indulged in weird orgies with his bathing-suited victims before slaying them.

Oak Lake Burial Witness Questioned. Game Warden Earl Bowers had arrested Harvey Staples of Wydota on charges of illegal muskrat trapping at Oak Lake. Staples, when brought to the Milquevais County jail, had volunteered a statement to Sheriff William Popke. It had been Harvey's practice to run his trapline before daylight, and before daybreak of a morning a week before Christmas he had observed an automobile proceeding without lights across the Oak Lake ice.

I remembered Staples. He was one of the carp-seining crew. In fact, the picture of him on the *Globe's* front page had been blown up from my photo of the six fishermen. The camera had caught a thin grin on his beard-shadowed hatchet face.

Sifting though Les Jopperman's prose, though, I found only vague details. Harvey Staples hadn't observed the automobile's make or model; he had only overheard a motor running in the darkness. The illegal trapper had figured a car without lights might belong to a game warden, and he had taken to his heels.

If it had been the murderer's car, that meant the body had been in the lake nearer six or seven weeks than two or three.

Or it meant Harvey Staples hoped the State would drop the muskrat charges if he testified in a murder trial.

On Monday came the home-town's Saturday head-line:

VICTIM IDENTIFIED; WAS CO-OP EMPLOYEE. On Friday evening Ralph Riker had viewed the remains in the Milquevais Mortuary Chapel and had recog-nized the Oak Lake girl as Gladys Irvine, twenty-seven, until recently employed as electronics com-puter operator at the Farmers Cooperative Creamery. The *Globe* quoted Riker:

"Gladys Irivine roomed and boarded in our home, located at 1812 Superior Street," Mr. Riker said in a statement to County Attorney Walter Burch.

"It just never entered our head she could be the one, though. She quit her job the last day of Decem-ber. Her reason was, she wanted to be closer to her sister in Minneapolis.

"There was all the talk about the dead girl being in the lake two or three weeks, and then the talk it might have been from before Christmas. The first suspicion struck me when I remembered Gladys let her hair down when she had a headache.

"She had a headache the night of December 31st. Jessie had cooked a meal of steak, French fries, broc-coli, and ice cream and cake, and Gladys didn't eat a bite. She stayed in her room, saying she had a nervous headache from the packing.

"I put her two suitcases in the car before I walked

down to the bowling alley. Mrs. Riker dropped Gladys off at the station on her way to pick me up around 9:30. We went home and I got dressed up and we went to the Hegglands' to celebrate the New Year.

"I feel morally certain the body is that of Gladys Irvine. She had peculiar, crowded teeth. . . ."

The story thus far was written in Ed Horace's straight style—he had batted out the lead and then filled in with the verbatim statement. In fact, he had probably stepped across the street to the courthouse and assembled his story on a typewriter in Walter Burch's office, consulting the stenographic record as he worked.

Reading it, I ransacked my memory for a recollection of Gladys Irvine.

I remembered vague glimpses of a pudgy, dumpy, plain-faced woman in the Co-op business office who'd worn her light-colored hair in a tight bun that could have intensified headaches.

She was the ponytailed blonde?

I read on. While Ed Horace covered my courthouse beat, Leslie Jopperman had been out at 1812 Superior Street, interviewing Mrs. Riker.

"Gladys Irvine lived in our midst as a woman of mystery, cloaked in reticences through which flashed occasional glimpses of a haunted and terror-pursued spirit," Leslie had written. "During working hours she functioned with much of the mechanical efficiency of the electronic automaton she tended. At home, after sharing the evening repast with Mr. and

Mrs. Riker, Gladys customarily chose to retire to the solitude of her upstairs room. At first, supposing the young woman to be homesick in her new surroundings, the Rikers sought to share with her the simple pleasures of wholesome Milquevais living, such as bowling, attending the movies, and motoring to the nearby lakes. Gladys always declined, pleading weariness or a headache.

"When the Rikers went out for an evening, they invariably returned to find the doors and windows of their home locked and bolted, and Gladys locked in her room. In reply to their questions, Gladys confessed to an obsessive fear of burglars.

" 'I asked her what she would do if a man broke in while she was alone in the house,' Jessica Riker related to this reporter. 'She replied that she kept a large and loaded pistol for protection. Then, bursting into tears, she described how, when only three years of age, she had seen her father slain in cold blood by a hold-up man.'

"Mrs. Riker expressed the belief that this childhood tragedy left psychological scars that Gladys carried to her ice-hewn grave. It might even be said that the wretched young woman suffered the presentiment of an untimely and violent end.

"Yet the nature of Gladys Irvine had its sunnier and even optimistic side.

"During the past summer, Gladys spent her week ends with her sister in Minneapolis. She traveled by the 9:30 Friday night train and returned by the Sunday midnight express, always leaving in a mood of happy anticipation and coming back exhausted but exhilarated by the trip. The change was marked by her dieting to lose weight, employing a bleaching rinse upon her hair, and in a general improvement of her personal appearance.

"While Jessica Riker refrained from asking tactless questions, she felt that Gladys and the sister had been estranged by a family quarrel and that a reconciliation had resulted in the new-found happiness.

"Then, at summer's end, the week-end trips ceased and Gladys again put on weight and resumed her solitary and brooding existence. 'In my alarm for Gladys' condition, I was tempted to write or telephone the sister,' Mrs. Riker said during the interview. 'I would have done so, only Gladys never did confide in me her sister's name and address. However, Gladys went to the Cities over Thanksgiving, and I believe at that time the two made it up. Anyway, two or three weeks later, a woman came to our door and said she was Gladys' sister and went up to Gladys' room. They talked for a couple of hours, and the next day Gladys told me she was going to give notice to the Co-op on account of the sister's health. The sister was a pale woman under her makeup, blonder than Gladys, and taller.

" 'I never knew Gladys to wear her hair down except after washing it, which she did in the basement. I don't even know if she owned a bathing suit. I bought one at Crane's sale and told her what a bargain it was, but I doubt if Gladys shopped downtown a dozen times in the two years she lived here.

" 'I last saw her standing on the railroad platform beside her two suitcases waiting for the ticket window to open. She had a dread of being late for trains. I often used to drive her to the train on account of the distance we live from the station.

" 'Looking back on my last glimpse of her, I now realize she made a figure of affliction and tragedy which at the time I ascribed to her headache coupled with her natural worries for her sister's health. Just before leaving our home for the last time she went to the refrigerator and took a glass of milk and may have nibbled a piece of bread.' "

The *Globe* also carried a boxed front-page statement issued by Olin Wolff:

"The long-established policy of the Co-op is to employ local people whenever they can be found to possess the necessary qualifications. Miss Irvine came to us as a factory-trained representative to train Mrs. Riker in the operation of the computer. The machine needed continual adjustments, and finally we employed Miss Irvine on a permanent basis. She did not quit her job, but requested an indefinite leave of absence to attend to her personal affairs. We will promote Mrs. Riker to the position and seek a local girl as assistant. The pressure of preparing the annual report makes it difficult to break in a new employee at the present time. Applicants are respectfully requested to await notification of a job opening."

There was also Olin Wolff's statement on the second page:

"I wish on this occasion to express the deep sense of loss felt by all of us who knew and worked side by side with Miss Irvine. She was one of those devoted and dedicated persons who avoid the limelight, the kind of good and faithful servant whose services are insufficiently appreciated by the community at large or by the far-flung members of such an organization as ours. Speaking from my own intimate experience of the administrative complexities involved in the management of the Co-op, I venture to predict Miss Irvine will be increasingly missed in the days to come."

Finally, Sheriff Popke had questioned Clifford Daly, the Mud Hen's Milquevais agent. Mr. Daly could not remember selling a ticket to Gladys Irvine on the night of December thirty-first. Miss Irvine and her suitcases seemed to have simply melted into the thin air.

On Monday I made the usual fruitless trip to Tijuana; Monday evening I came back and found the practical nurse gone and Kelly's mother out of the cast and getting around with the help of a cane. I told her the usual lies.

Tuesday morning came the Milquevais Monday sensation:

DEAD GIRL LINKED TO MILK CHECK FRAUDS. Attorney Walter Burch was studying evidence indicating Gladys Irvine's possible implication in a large-scale defalcation of Farmers Cooperative Creamery funds. He described the evidence as consisting of nine milk checks made payable to unknown or fictitious individuals, the checks ranging from $94.15 to $426.25, amounting to in all $2581.60.

Olin Wolff declared that the spurious checks were the product of the Co-op's electronic computer. "Every farmer belonging to the organization has an account number," the treasurer had explained. "Holes are punched in the member's card, and the cards are run through the computer. However, in an organization as large as ours, every month a few members die or retire. It appears the account numbers of former members were used to cause the machine to issue these fictitious checks."

The checks were all dated the tenth of December, presumably in payment of November milk collections.

"The Co-op has for years made a policy of cashing checks for its members," Olin Wolff further explained. "Some farmers are too busy to get to town during banking hours. They bring their checks in here, and we cash them. The checks bearing the payee's endorsement and the Co-op's rubber stamp are then forwarded to the First National Bank to be credited to the Co-op account."

County Attorney Burch described the swindle as an ingenious one that guaranteed the perpetrator a month's head start of detection. "The First National closes its books on the twenty-fifth of each month," he said. "Deposits and withdrawals occurring after that date are entered on the succeeding month's statement. The fraudulent checks were processed on

December 29, 30, and 31. They were accepted without question at the bank, and were subsequently returned to the Co-op along with the January bank statement. They were again run through the computer for distribution to the appropriate accounts. Mrs. Riker happened to notice that a check bearing account number 3004, belonging to a Mr. Alvin Mork of Goodlands, in fact bore the name of one Leo Holtz. Mrs. Riker, fearing the computer was out of adjustment, called the matter to the attention of Swedenborg Wolff. Being notified of the circumstances, I proceeded to the Co-op, and, working most of Saturday night with the assistance of Mrs. Riker and Swedenborg Wolff, discovered the eight additional fraudulent checks."

Burch said that persisting efforts to locate a sister of Gladys Irvine's in Minneapolis had led to the discovery that Miss Irvine was in fact the only child of a Mrs. Eugenia Irvine.

"Eugenia Irvine died in Minneapolis in 1956," the prosecutor had said. "Her probated will mentions only the one daughter, Gladys. Eugenia was the widow of a Charles Irvine, who was killed in a radio store holdup in 1934. The newspaper reports at the time stated he was survived by his wife and the one child, Gladys.

"Gladys Irvine appears to have given the Wolffs and the Rikers false explanations of her movements and her reasons for leaving the Co-op's employ.

"Gladys Irvine was the one who normally produced the Co-op checks.

"Gladys Irvine had access to the vault in which the Co-op cash was kept.

"The investigation opens the possibility that Gladys Irvine at the time of her death had in her possession in excess of twenty-five hundred dollars taken from the vault on December 29, 30, and 31."

The story had the standardized flavor and texture of store bread, and I found myself missing the spice-and-raisins of Les Jopperman's style of journalism. What had happened to Les's usually agile imagination? How come he'd failed to cook up a theory that Gladys Irvine had lived in Milquevais as a woman in hiding, that her reducing and hair-bleaching and ponytail represented efforts to alter her appearance drastically, that she had taken the money to finance a flight from peril?

Why hadn't Les served up Gladys as the victim of a blackmailer, driven to committing theft to satisfy the demands of an extortionist?

Kelly's mother brought me back to realities with a thud. She did so by hobbling out of her bedroom, wearing a hat and a blue cloth coat and grasping her cane in a white-gloved hand.

"Kenneth, I've decided it's best for me to accompany you to Tijuana today."

What had become of my own agile imagination?

"Well, fine, Mother Kelly. Only of course you realize I'm driving this little car, a little tricky to get in and out of. I guess it'd be better to wait and let the bone knit a day or so more."

Mrs. Kelly looked at me awhile. I felt like the

drowning man whose life unreels in reverse before his eyes, and I was back to the stage of six-year-old delinquency when she spoke again.

"All right, Kenneth, now be honest and tell me the *real* reason."

"It's the jail. Kelly's up on the second floor, and the steps are steep and narrow, practically like climbing a ladder—"

The *purr* of the telephone came to my rescue. I rushed to it.

"Senor Svederup?"

I recognized Gaitterez's voice. "Yeah, speaking, *buenos dias*. What's up?"

"I have the honor of informing you that Senora Svederup is among the first eight prisoners eligible for bail—"

"It's okay, Mother, Kelly's out!"

Gaitterez was saying something at the other end of the wire.

"I'll be right down, take me less than an hour," I said.

"Effective tomorrow, not today."

"Look, Gaitterez, this isn't some more of the old *manana* runaround?" The feeling of being reprieved was already going down the drain.

"Our justice is unhurried; certain papers must be processed; and in the majority of cases no doubt time will be required to make the financial arrangements. The bail has been set in the amount of sixteen hundred dollars."

"How much is that in U.S. money?"

"Hello? One thousand, six hundred dollars," said Senor Gaitterez. "In our currency, twenty thousand pesos."

And I had thought he was giving me the good news.

"Hello, Senor Svederup? Can you hear me?"

"I can hear you, and don't you think it's one hell of a stiff rap?"

"Our laws are stiff. The judge took into account the severity of the offense and the affront to our national institutions."

Yes, and he took into account I could not possibly let Kelly rot in the jail or be committed to the penitentiary.

But, sixteen hundred bucks!

I left behind the Kelly's middle-class neighborhood and followed a climbing street through a younger, rising neighborhood of oleanders and tulip trees and power-clipped lawns surrounding two-story Mediterranean homes. The pavement ahead clung to a canyon rim, and to the canyonside clung eyebrows of extremely modernistic architecture having sloping shed roofs studded with plastic bubbles, surrounded by plantings of exotic bamboo and plumed grasses. This petered out into native brush and manzanita, and after that I came to old H. H. Crossway's top-of-the-world estate.

Since I'd last been up here, the wall surrounding the property had been pink-painted. The same wall-top plantings of cacti stabbed needles into the sun-

light. The same contact plates in the driveway
opened and closed the ornamental steel gate. The
driveway, lined by Crossway's pet rose bushes,
curved through a glistening grove of lime, orange,
and lemon trees. The centerpiece consisted of a half-
acre barbered lawn, a skating-rink-sized swimpool,
and a half-timbered chateau only slightly smaller
than the Milquevais courthouse.

The whole layout made sixteen hundred dollars
look like a ten-cent tip. I parked under the suspicious
stare of a workman lopping down poinsettia canes.
He waited with machete in hand while I thumbed
the bell button and until a white-capped and white-
aproned maid appeared and gave me a half-remem-
bering glance.

"Why, it's Mr. Sheerdrop, isn't it?" she said.

"Svederup," I said.

Fifteen or twenty poinsettia canes fell in the time
it took the maid to go and find out that Mr. Crossway
would receive me in his study.

The Old Man's study was a tycoon's nest furnished
with a dark-wood directors' table and leather-cush-
ioned chairs, trophy cases full of loving cups, gold
medals, and blue ribbons won by his prize rose
bushes, mementos of his dead son Junior, and a news-
ticker just like the one at the Milquevais *Globe*.
There was also the Old Man, eroded by the fifteen
years since his *Globe* wall photo was taken and re-
touched. He looked like the yellowed ivory king on a
mahogany and gold-inlaid chessboard, the last piece
on the board.

There was nothing on the directors' table except a humidor of cigars and a silver bowl full of his newest hybrid rose creation, big blood red blooms as perfect as those you see in the seed catalogues.

The Old Man remembered me, offered a cigar as an excuse for helping himself to one, went on from there to introduce me to the new champion rose: "I want you to meet the Stanley Yankus."

I was more interested in getting my wife out of Mexico and told him so.

No surprise slackened the Old Man's time-wasted jaw. "Oh, that. I noticed something in the local press." He knew Kelly was my wife; he'd seen her name in the news accounts; but he wasn't handing out any condolences. Instead he lectured, "You have to take the long-range view of events. Actually a Mexican Monte Carlo right across the border would only serve to siphon off the American working man's wage and the tourist dollar. Also, the U.S. Government is engaged in negotiations for air rights giving access to a contemplated landing field adjoining the International Line—" The Old Man's silvered brows scowled over faded blue-denim eyes. "You're a bright young fellow, Svederup. With seasoning, you could become upper-echelon timber. But you keep failing the test of objectivity—you let your judgment be swayed by emotion, and to me emotionalism in a newspaperman is a worse disease than alcoholism."

"Right now I'm more interested in Kelly's future

than mine," I said, "and it's going to cost sixteen hundred dollars to bail her out of jail."

The old denim eyes followed a smoke ring toward the study ceiling.

"I haven't got the cash, Mr. Crossway. I left home with nine hundred dollars. Out of that I bought a plane ticket, and I have to pay a Tijuana lawyer for handling the case. I need another thousand by to-morrow morning."

This was the most objective speech I ever made in my life, and the most bitterly emotional, too.

"You want my advice?" said H. H. Crossway.

"I want the loan of the thousand, and I will pay it back at the rate of ten or fifteen dollars a week from my salary."

The Old Man might have been counting to ten. At the end of the countdown he blew a smoke dough-nut at the ceiling. It might have been a moon shot from his absorbed interest in the smoke ring's as-cent. Two-thirds of way to the target, the thing fell apart.

"My advice is this," he said. "Let Mrs. Sverderup sit it out another week and undoubtedly the Mexi-can authorities will reduce the bail by half."

He was right, as it turned out. And even without waiting to see how it turned out, I had the feeling he was right.

"At six per cent interest," I said.

"And if she will sit tight for two weeks, and plead hardship, they will cut the reduced bail in half again."

Right once more, and I knew it. But I said, "You haven't seen the jail."

"She'd be saving you approximately a hundred dollars a day the first week and approximately fifty a day the second week."

"I can't let Kelly spend an unnecessary hour in that tank, and I won't."

H. H. Crossway removed his cigar from his mouth, turned it in his arthritically gnarled fingers, and seemed to be deciphering a coded message on its dappled Havana skin.

"I started life as an advertising card salesman," he reminisced. "I had saved up $125, and Mrs. Crossway needed a winter coat. We talked it over and decided to buy a second-hand press to print the cards on. Mrs. Crossway ran the press in the basement, and I sold the cards. We saved $750. We could have bought a car, but we talked it over and decided to make the down payment on a job printing shop. The job shop earned the price of the first Crossway paper, and the first paper saved the price of the next two, and I've noticed the men with the extravagant wives stay reporters all their lives. So I advise you to sit down and talk this over with Mrs. Svederup."

"It's impossible," I said. "The money doesn't mean that much to me. It doesn't mean that much to Kelly. And there's Kelly's mother—she can't afford it after the doctor bills, but I know positively she'd second-mortgage her home to raise the bail. Anyway, I'm not going to let my wife and my mother-in-law take the rap."

The Old Man opened a drawer under the directors' tabletop, lifted out a ledger-sized checkbook, unclipped a pen from his coat pocket. He made out the check, hesitated before tearing the perforated paper, hesitated some more before handing me the oblong slip. "This goes against my grain. I know perfectly well I'm aiding and abetting you in making an emotional damned fool of yourself."

"Thanks a lot just the same, Mr. Crossway."

"The time will come when you won't thank me, and your wife won't thank me or you either."

The next morning I reached Senior Gaitterez's office ahead of Senor Gaitterez. We both reached the courtroom ahead of anybody with the authority to accept the bail-release form and the money. It was nearly noon before a pair of uniformed court attendants consented to count my bankroll.

They counted it four times, looking at both sides of every bill every time. It came at sixteen hundred dollars, all right.

"There is required $2.50 additional, *senor*."

"*No sabe*," said I.

"It is the fee for changing your dollars into pesos," said Senor Gaitterez.

The $1602.50 bought me a stamped and certified receipt that I could exchange for Kelly at the federal penitentiary—it was contrary to the code and the national institutions to let her just walk out of jail.

Senor Gaitterez gave me a sketched map showing where to find the penitentiary, and I gave him one hundred dollars for his services. He charged me no fee for changing the money into Mexican currency.

At the end of a ten-mile drive, I found the penitentiary.

It got to be one o'clock; it got to be two o'clock; it got to be three o'clock.

Behind the Renault five other cars were lined up, each with California plates, each containing friends or relatives of jailed Americans. One of these, a gaunt-faced citizen of Long Beach, told me he was awaiting the release of his brother. "I was in a Jap prison-a-war camp myself. I swear tuh Gawd, this Mex hoosegow stinks worse and is dirtier than the Jap camp."

Along came a brown-faced, straw-sombreroed man to sell me an enchilada from a glass box on push-cart wheels.

"Don't touch any of their grub," the Long Beachite advised me. "You want to die of dysentery?"

"Well, if the germs are as slow as the national institutions, I'll live to a ripe old age."

At four-thirty a car containing the first batch of released prisoners pulled through a side gate. Kelly, carrying her handbag and a pair of folded blankets, trudged across the prison yard and emerged from another gate.

"Where were you born?" said the U.S. Immigration patrolman at the border entry check.

"In God's country!" said Kelly.

"You folks buy anything in Mexico?" inquired the Customs inspector.

"Yes! Freedom!" Kelly twisted around in the seat to face me. "I've been saving up those answers for a week!" She burst into tears.

"That's all over now," and I started an arm around her shoulders.

"Don't, Ken, please don't—I won't feel human until I've had a bath. The best we could manage was a sponge-off while the others held up blankets."

Somehow the drive to La Jolla seemed more in the mood of a funeral procession than a triumphant return.

Mother Kelly, with the cane in one hand and cooking with the other, had prepared a dinner of oven-fried chicken, escalloped potatoes, and artichokes that had to wait while Kelly shampooed and hot-tubbed, and called from the bathroom:

"Ken, run down to the drugstore for some calamine lotion—I'm all over bites."

We sat down to dinner an hour late, Kelly in an old bathrobe, the visible parts of her smeared with the calamine, barely able to keep her eyes open long enough to swallow a few mouthfuls. "I haven't had anything but catnaps for a week," she said, and staggered off to bed.

I cleared the table and washed and dried the dishes and went to bed early myself. In the guest room.

Falling asleep was something else.

I knew perfectly well Kelly wasn't *that* dirty or *that* tired, and she had been bitten worse by mosquitoes on Milquevais picnics.

In Kelly's case, a psychological reaction had occurred.

I thought about that, and I also thought about
one thousand dollars at six per cent divided by fifteen dollars a week. We would be a year and a half
paying the debt, and at the end of the year and a half
we would still be nine hundred dollars worse off than
when all this started. It'd be three years before we
got caught up.

It wasn't the money; it was the three years.

I closed my eyes and tried counting sheep, and
woke up from a doze realizing the sheep had changed
into golden-scaled carp freezing on the Oak Lake ice.

"Good golly," I thought, "maybe at that Les and
I could work up an entry in the *Bloody Murder Magazine* contest and split the first prize."

The idea pulled me out of bed, into the front room
in search of the morning's mail. I tore the airmail
wrapper from yesterday's Milquevais *Globe:*

REWARD POSTED FOR IRVINE SLAYER. A five-thou-
sand-dollar reward for information leading to the
arrest and conviction of the person or persons responsible for the murder of Gladys Irvine had
been announced by County Attorney Walter Burch.
Burch said a certified check for that amount had
been tendered to the prosecutor's office by James T.
Holadare, an executive of the Holadare Company of
Minneapolis, manufacturers of an electronic computing device used in the Farmers Cooperative
Creamery treasurer's department. Mr. Holadare,

following a three-hour conference with the local county attorney, coroner, and sheriff, declared that the company could not remain indifferent to the charge that Miss Irvine, a factory-trained representative of the concern, had engaged in systematic looting of Co-op funds.

"The company's position was decided at an emergency meeting of the board of directors," Mr. Holadare had declared. "The decision was to run to earth whoever profited from the production and cashing of the fraudulent checks. If accomplices were involved, the company means to do all in its power to bring them to justice. If, on the other hand, Miss Irvine's death and the thefts are separate and unrelated crimes, we mean to bring that fact to light."

Five thousand dollars!

I stumbled back to bed and lay there counting clues.

NINE

The plane bored along on top of broken clouds; the breaks in the clouds gave glimpses of winter prairie cut into mile-square sections by country roads, the sections subdivided into fields and pastures by fence lines. From the clouds fell snow flurries, and over the farmyards and small towns and occasional lakes raced thin, smoky veils of whiteness.

"Why so glum?" demanded Kelly.

"I'm thinking—"

"Would it be going too far to ask about what?"

"My novel. It's a well-known fact that writers do their most important work just sitting and looking out windows."

In fact, I was still adding up clues in the Gladys Irvine case. It seemed to me these clues sorted into two separate columns. In one column were the circumstances related in the *Globe*—Gladys' habit of locking herself in her upstairs bedroom at the Rikers', her week-end visits with a nonexistent sister, her periodic bouts of reducing, the coincidental disappearance of the Co-op's funds and the vanishing of Gladys from the Milquevais railroad station platform. In another column were *"Valhalla,"* Midge Holadare, Dirk Lebijohn, and the slugging in the *Globe* parking lot. Added separately, they gave different answers. Added together, they equaled nonsense.

"You're lying, Ken," said Kelly in a lowered, strained, vehement tone. "You're keeping something from me."

That was true, but I didn't want to arouse in Kelly any premature hopes of successfully claiming the five thousand reward. It has always seemed to me that the time to talk about a satellite launching is *after* you've got the bird in orbit.

"Is it possible you're secretly jealous of Roy Elling?" Kelly went on.

I studied her face. It was strangely whitened, and I got the impression her lips were bloodless under the lipsticking. I got another impression—that her eyes were tearlessly crying.

"I'm not jealous. I trust you, for God's sake."

"Or you don't care, and you take me for granted—"

What was all this?

"I don't say I wasn't a little jealous, subconsciously, just at first. Until I found out Elling is just a kid, and Leah Wilson's kid brother at that."

Kelly grimaced.

"What's the matter?" I said.

"The question isn't what you think of Roy Elling; it's what you think of me. And I gather you think I'm perfectly contented with being a Milquevais *Hausfrau*, perfectly happy being cooped up in the house five months a year. Actually, jail wasn't such a new experience, and all I can see ahead is more solitary confinement. Doing the dishes, making the bed, with a daily outdoor exercise period to shop for groceries and lug home another armful of public library novels."

I might have remarked I was the one who urged her to break the monotony by the Christmas trip to California, but what had to be faced was the future. "It isn't La Jolla, I admit, but Milquevais isn't so bad—"

"*You're* satisfied. You have your job. You get around; you have your hunting and fishing."

"We'll have to do more fun things, then. Get to the Cities and see some of the shows—" Though with fifteen dollars missing from the weekly pay check, the splurging would be limited.

Anyway, Kelly sat shaking her head. "No, that's the typical man's solution. You seem to think an ailing marriage can be cured by pretending to be single again, by taking me out on a date as you used to. Flowers, candy, tickets to a show, and then a big passionate pass. I'm sorry, but an occasional date of that kind isn't the answer for us."

Into the aftermath of dismal silence I said, "Things will work out, Kelly," but I didn't say how. I didn't know how.

The plane slid under the scudding clouds and in the teeth of fine-flying snow made its Minneapolis airport landing. There was the usual delay unloading the luggage, and I got hold of a phonebook. It listed

James Holadare, 2525 Paul Bunyan Lane, Larksdale. James Holadare was the only entry in both columns of clues. I rang the Larksdale number.

"Hello?" a woman's voice caroled.

"Mrs. Holadare?"

"Speaking."

"This is Ken Svederup of Milquevais."

The wires between hummed faintly.

"Hello?" I said.

"Yes," said the voice, several flute notes higher, "what do you want?"

"Want to drop in and chat a few moments."

"You mean this evening? I'm afraid that won't be convenient. I'm expecting my husband home any time now—"

"Your husband is the one I want to chat with."

The wire hummed awhile. "I'm sorry, but I can't promise when he'll be in. Jim often works late—"

"Later will be fine. I'll catch dinner on the way."

"Later we have some friends dropping in."

"Mrs. Svederup and I won't stay long."

"Mrs.—! What have you told her?"

"What you told Mr.," I said. "I've been a little tongue-tied recently. The result of a head injury."

The wire was humming again when I hung up.

Next, I put through a reverse-charge call to the *Globe* in Milquevais. Leo Spenser, the photo and engraving lab man, answered. "Horace went home early," he said. "He's got the flu, a temperature of 103."

"Is Les Jopperman around, then?" I said.

"Les Jopperman quit in a huff."

"Over what?"

"I understand he dug up something libelous, and Horace refused to print it."

"Tell me more."

"I don't know any more—I'm just sitting night-hawk on the news-ticker. Unless Russia calls off the cold war, something like that, we're going to press with the big news that Harvey Staples is out on bail. Ralph Riker put up the bail."

"What are you laughing about, Leo?"

"Funny thing about Harvey Staples. I'll tell you —*show* you—when you get back. When will you?"

I told Leo I had to eat dinner, wanted to see James Holadare about the background of the reward offer, and would probably pull into Milquevais around nine-thirty or ten.

Through a thin driving of fine, powdery snow, I trudged to the nearby garage, where I'd put up the Chevie, headed back to the airport, and picked up Kelly and the luggage. It'd stopped snowing when we pulled into a roadside restaurant, but it was snowing again when we came out.

Larksdale was a recent and labyrinthine sub-division, built up around a golf course—the kind of place where they throw in a country-club member-ship with the deed to the lot. Entering the labyrinth, I turned into a Mother Goosey filling station. The attendant said straight ahead to the golf course and take the right turn opposite the number-five hole. These directions brought us to a dead-end stop in

front of a former hip-roofed red barn converted into
an amateur playhouse. A man unloading a bass
drum from a Volkswagen said go back and turn left
after crossing the bridge. After some argument as to
whether we'd crossed a bridge or merely a culvert, we
finally did track the Holadares to their split-level
lair.

"But this is *nice*," said Kelly, looking over the lair.

"Did you expect a hovel?"

"I expected something pretentious, but this is
just *nice*. I'm going to be interested to see the inside."

We advanced up a walk cleared of snow by the
wind. Midge Holadare answered the door. She had
her red hair piled up in a style that bared her ears.
She wore tiny green brilliant earrings, a throat-high
and wrist-long demure white dress, and a wedding
ring. No engagement ring. I figured she hadn't told
James Holadare about finding it.

She said, "Jim knows a reporter phoned and was
on the way out. He's in the kitchen mixing Martinis
for the party. Won't you come along?"

She did not suggest we take off our wraps.

We stepped from the entry hall into a living room
aglow with small scattered lamps. Kelly stopped
short.

"It's charming." She looked around at the eggshell
white walls and wine-toned draperies and open fire
snapping in the small tile-enclosed fireplace.

"We like it," Midge Holadare said. "Of course,
there are things I could do without." She flicked a

glance at me and then at an oil painting above the mantel. "Mother Holadare," she murmured.

A modern blonde-wood frame tried to take the curse off the gloom tones of a silver-haired dowager seated in a thronelike chair. Something about the portrait reminded me of the H. H. Crossway photo in Ed Horace's office. Mother Holadare's eyes seemed to follow us as we descended to a lower level and a dining room large enough to seat eight. It would have seated twelve but for the formidable provincial breakfront taking up the whole end wall.

"Mother Holadare's Christmas gift," said Midge.

Kelly said the dining room was charming. We entered the kitchen. The kitchen took away Kelly's breath.

Personally, I looked at James Holadare. I guessed he took after his father instead of Mother Holadare. He was a cowlick-thatched chap of about thirty-five, tall enough to have played college basketball. Under the cowlick he had a face as thin and scholastic as a Phi Beta Kappa key. He wore a Norfolk jacket, slacks, and loafers. To me he looked like a member of the Made Generation, an intellectual who should have gone in for research instead of a business career.

I could have been misled by his method of mixing Martinis. He was flowing the ingredients into a Rube Goldberg apparatus of glass pipes and glass bulbs—"blending without shaking or stirring," he explained.

I told him who I was, that I'd be covering the

Gladys Irvine case from here on, and I wondered why the Holadare Company cared five thousand dollars' worth about Gladys.

Midge broke in. "The reward was Mother Holadare's idea," she said. "You see, Jim's father founded the company back in the twenties. He disappeared at the time of the 1929 stock market crash—went out for a walk and vanished like Judge Crater. In 1930 Mother Holadare sued for divorce on grounds of desertion, and later she had Charles Holadare declared legally dead. It seems divorce didn't void the will, and the will left her fifty-one per cent of the company stock."

All this the redhead delivered with the speed of a television announcer making the most of a station break.

"Mother Holadare's whim is law," she continued. "If she wanted to offer a million-dollar reward, Jim and everybody else in the company would have to go along."

James Holadare peered from under his cowlick at his wife. He said very quietly, "My dear, I'm sure Mrs. Svederup would enjoy seeing the rest of the house."

"I doubt if she's interested," said his wife.

"Oh, but I am, and I'd love to," said Kelly.

"Sure," I said, "show her the house."

Midge Holadare went out, followed by Kelly. James Holadare said to me, "My father left behind a small business in shaky financial condition. My mother put the company on its feet, and during

World War II obtained some electronic equipment contracts, and after the war pioneered in the commercial electronics computing field. Do you know how a computer works?"

I didn't.

"A computer counts on its fingers, but it has millions of fingers and counts with the speed of electricity. However, the facts you feed into it have to be broken down into simple digital form. Take for instance the Farmers Cooperative Creamery in Milquevais. The problem there was to break down the factors of so many pounds of milk divided by so many percentages used as butterfat, used in ice cream, in cottage cheese, and in dried-milk powders, the percentages varying from week to week and the base prices varying from day to day."

"I still don't get it," I said, "and what difference does it make?"

"The point is, our computer isn't a standardized product like a typewriter or adding machine. It has to be adjusted, set up to suit the needs of the user. It's one deal in a creamery, another deal in a hospital, another in a municipal tax office." James Holadare broke off. "How about a sample?"

"Fine," I said.

He crossed to a refrigerator, got out ice cubes, and put the cubes through an ice chopper on the stainless-steel sink drainboard. He kept talking.

"It's called statistical systems analysis, and it took me four years at the U and two postgrad years to learn it," he said. "I think you can see statistical systems analysis is impossible unless the client opens his books in a perfectly frank manner. You can't break the operation down into digital simplicity unless you know how the business is run, how the books are kept. That's where Gladys came in."

"Where?"

"When we install a computer, we send along a factory-trained representative to make sure the machine is really set up to do the job."

"You make Gladys sound like a regular little Miss Einstein."

"Oh, no. She worked under me, and referred any complicated problems to me."

"Then you knew her pretty well?"

James Holadare filled a pair of Martini glasses and handed one to me.

"Skoal," said he.

"Cheers," said I.

"How well does anyone know anyone else, really?" he continued. "You can live in the same house with another human being and one day find out you don't know that person so very well."

"You can say that again."

"Gladys had been with the company three or four years. She seemed to be a quiet, conscientious, dependable girl who performed her functions in an efficient manner. But it isn't Gladys my mother cares so much about."

"Oh?"

"My mother feels that business outfits are not going to confide their methods and operations to the

Holadare Company, not if they feel our factory-trained representatives are going to spot flaws in the setup and grab the chance of embezzling money."

"I see."

"My mother's idea is to prove to the business world that the Holadare Company will go to any lengths to prosecute any employee or former employee who is guilty of pulling a fast one. She thinks doing so will help keep other girls like Gladys honest."

A telephone on the kitchen wall rang.

"Extension," James Holadare said. "Midge will get it."

The phone rang again.

"And if Gladys had an accomplice," James Holadare said, "we want to prevent the accomplice from trying the same stunt again."

The telephone rang a third time.

He decided to take the call, crossed to the wall, and held the receiver to his ear.

"It's for *you,*" he said a moment later.

I stepped to his side and held the receiver to my ear. "Speaking," I said.

The voice that came over the wire sounded like a cross between Ed Horace's normal tones and a bull-frog's croak.

"Ken, Leo said you might be there. I want you to drop it and head for Milquevais as fast as you can. Hell is to pay here."

"What's happened?"

"The Rikers have disappeared, and it looks like foul play."

A sound of coughing came over the wire. Then Ed went on to feed me the story in experienced legman style.

"Mrs. Riker worked as usual at the Co-op today," he said. "She left at five to go home and fix dinner for herself and Ralph, after which she was supposed to go back to the office and put in some overtime on the annual report. She didn't return, and Swede Wolff couldn't raise her on the phone. Swede went to the house and found the table set, the meal cooked and waiting on the stove. The Rikers and their car are missing. The question is, Why would they rush away just when they were ready to sit down to the table, and without a word to anyone? Willie Popke is out there now investigating it. I'm leaving for the office now, going to hold the paper to the last possible minute. You should be able to make the drive in two hours, in time to help if we have to remake the front page."

"All right, Ed," I said.

The clock on the Holadare kitchen wall said seven twenty-three.

"I have to leave," I said to James Holadare.

"One for the road?" he asked cordially.

The sound of chimes tinkled from the front of the house.

"Midge will get that," Holadare said. "You have time for one for the road, and besides, there's one more small point I'd like to make."

"What's that?"

He refilled the glasses.

"Cheers," he said.

"Skoal," I said.

"The small point is simply this: Gladys Irvine may not be responsible for that check business. The Riker woman had the same chance. So had Swedenborg Wolff. So, for that matter, had Olin Wolff himself. We don't know who-all at some hour of the day or night had access to the computing equipment. As a matter of fact, the defalcation may actually have occurred at the First National Bank instead of in the Co-op treasurer's office."

He reminded me of a hunter scatter-gunning a flock of mallards, hoping to drop any bird at all. The explanation may have been the entrance of Midge Holadare and Kelly.

"Oh, goody, drinks," said Midge.

"The Svederups are just leaving, dear," Holadare said. "I'll step out to the car with you, Svederup." It sounded as if he wanted to steer me away from further conversation with his wife.

The redhead looked around. "Who was at the door?"

"I thought you answered," said Holadare.

Kelly was saying to me, "It's a terrific house, Ken." Her eyes glowed as they had not glowed since the Tijuana experience.

"Jim, you go. Don't leave the guests standing on the doorstep." Midge was pouring herself a Martini.

James Holadare brushed past me and Kelly.

"The bathrooms are all-over carpeted," Kelly told me.

James Holadare passed from sight, and Midge Holadare came over and handed the Martini to Kelly. To me she said, "We have skeletons in the closets, too. Did Jim tell you the Holadare Company originally manufactured pinball machines? Did he tell you his father was financed by hoodlums? It's even possible Charles Holadare was taken for a ride, buried in a lake or river with his legs in kegs of cement." Midge was talking too fast to make much sense.

"Is there any reason Jim should have told me all that?" I asked.

"There's a reason he wouldn't. He's covering up for Mother Holadare. You should know the background of this woman who's offering five thousand dollars for the dope on Gladys Irvine."

A shouted exclamation rang through the house.

Midge Holadare was nearest the dining room door and reached it first. I overtook her and hurdled ahead up the split-level steps into the living room. Ahead, in the entry hall, I saw James Holadare bent double and dragging a body into view. The entry was full of flying snow. There was more snow powdering the body.

I recognized Ralph Riker, a pretzel-shaped corpse in a tightly buttoned blue overcoat with strips of adhesive tape binding his wrists and ankles.

TEN

We behaved like four people shaken out of deep sleep and still only half awake. James Holadare dropped the body and lurched to close the front door, and, having closed it, stood with his shoulders braced against it and his legs planted wide apart.

"Call a doctor, Midge," he said.

There was a telephone on an entry hallway table within a yard of him.

"The man is in rigor mortis," I said, studying Ralph Riker's face. A swollen expression of congestion seemed frozen on his "nice-looking-fella's" features.

"Call the police, then," James Holadare said.

Midge Holadare stood at my elbow and breathed noisily.

"I opened the door, and he must have been propped against it. He fell in at my feet," James Holadare said to nobody in particular.

"Stand aside," I said.

Holadare seemed not to hear.

"Stand aside. I'm going outside and have a look around."

At that, Kelly snared my other elbow. "Ken, you're not going to get mixed up in this. You'll be killed, too!"

I reasoned with Kelly. "There is no danger," I said. "People who dump bodies on doorsteps don't stand around outside waiting for the police to arrive."

Midge Holadare ran in the direction of the kitchen.

"If there's nobody outside, what's the use of you going outdoors?" said Kelly.

"I just want to have a look."

"Don't let him go," Kelly said to James Holadare.

Holadare detached himself from the door, dropped a long arm to the telephone, and uncradled the instrument. As he did so, a thin reproduction of his wife's fluty voice spilled into the entry hall. "Don't come," she was saying. "The party has been called off. Something has hap—"

"Midge!" Holadare shouted into the phone. "Get off the line!"

"We can't have our friends walking into a police investigation," the fluty voice said.

Holadare stepped over Ralph Riker's body and rushed toward the kitchen. All this while, Kelly clung to my sleeve with both hands.

Using the free hand, I began unbuttoning my topcoat. "It's my duty to cover the story," I said. "There may be footprints in the snow."

From the phone lying beside its cradle emerged dialing sounds followed by James Holadare's voice: "Mother? Something horrible has happened. I just now opened the front door and—"

I twisted out of the topcoat, leaving Kelly hanging onto an empty sleeve. "Eavesdrop!" I said to her, and wrenched open the front door and leaped outside.

There were no footprints on the still-wind-cleared walk.

But at the curb end of the walk, and just behind the Chevie wagon, sat a second car.

A shiver chased through me, although it was not a particularly cold night and although I felt certain Ralph Riker's murderer could not be tamely awaiting the law. It was pride that stopped me from turning around and retreating into the house.

Anyway, I trudged to the curb. The car was one of those imported jobs you almost have to go on all fours to look into. Looking in, I saw two fused forms with heads glued in a smooch.

I tapped on the glass. The figures came apart. The man was on my side. He pushed open the door and stepped out facing me. When he opened the car door, a bulb had come on inside, and the escaping light revealed Dirk Lebijohn, hatless but wearing the same trenchcoat. He recognized me, too.

"Well, you nosy son of a," he said.

"How long have you been sitting here?" I said.

"Is it some of your business?"

While we exchanged these remarks, a tall young woman made bulky by a fur coat had gotten out on the driver's side. Now she said, "Oh, shut up, Dirk, and come on."

"How long?" I repeated.

"Ten seconds," she flung, pulling Lebijohn in the direction of the house.

He went along willingly enough.

I got the flashlight from the station wagon's glove

compartment and played the beam upon the pavement. The curb had stopped a small drift of the fine powdery snow. It looked as if the imported car had pulled in on top of tire treads left by an earlier vehicle, but the snow lacked the body to hold a definite impression. I hunted up and down the street away, and all I learned was that the Larksdale lots ran to two-hundred-foot frontages, and that the nearest neighboring house was two lots away.

To my thumbing of the door button, James Holadare responded by opening the door a crack. "Better go around to the— Oh, you. Come on in."

I came in and at once observed that the top two buttons of Ralph Riker's overcoat were loosened.

"I looked for identification," said Holadare, blushing. The blush made him look boyish.

"At your mother's suggestion?" I asked.

He scowled. The scowl made him look juvenilely delinquent.

"Do you mind if I call my paper?" I put through another collect call. Again Leo answered, saying Ed Horace hadn't yet reached the *Globe* building. I told Leo that Ralph Riker had just been found dead at the James Holadare residence and gave him the address.

"What about Jessica?" Leo asked.

"I went out and looked. Apparently there are no other bodies in the vicinity. Tell Ed I'll be here awhile—how long I guess depends on the police."

James Holadare's expression was thoughtful. It made him look scientific and detached.

"Gladys lived with a Riker family," he said. "What do you think?"

"I think I could use another of your Martinis if you can spare it."

We returned to the kitchen. Midge Holadare pounced with the speed of electricity. "Mr. Svederup, you don't know anyone here. Eva Shelton, Mr. Svederup. Dirk Lebijohn, Mr. Svederup."

Eva Shelton was a carnally beautiful girl, nervously toying with the front of her bulky squirrel coat. "Oh, hello," she said to me. And to Midge, "I feel we should be running along—we're butting in here."

"We were invited." Dirk Lebijohn had peeled off his trenchcoat and draped it on a breakfast bar, where Kelly had placed my topcoat.

Dirk wore a double-breasted blue pencil-striped suit tailored with hand's breadth and deeply notched lapels—the style of twenty years ago. He also wore a lumberjack's checked shirt, no tie, and yesterday's whiskers.

"The party's called off, and the cops will be here any minute," Eva said.

"I've always wanted to be interrogated by the cops," said Dirk Lebijohn.

"I work for a living," said Eva. "I don't want to be up half the night playing cops and robbers."

"The company will understand," said James Holadare in a kindly voice. "After all, you knew Gladys as well as anyone, and perhaps you can throw some helpful light."

"What has knowing Gladys got to do with this?" said Eva.

"Svederup here says the body is that of Ralph Riker."

Eva removed the squirrel coat. Her blue knit dress clung to a tall figure filled out like Bardot's.

I took the coat. "How well did you know Gladys?"

"We shared an apartment for a few months after her mother died."

"What was she like?"

"She was different."

"In what way?"

"She was fat," said Eva, "and she didn't give a damn about dates and spent most of her time brooding over her mother's papers."

"What kind of papers?"

"Don't answer that," said Lebijohn in a loud, ugly voice.

I looked at him. His beard bristled out of discolored skin.

"Any information relating to Gladys Irvine is worth money," he said. "No reason Eva should give it to you, any more than she should give you that coat off her back."

I looked back to Eva. "The police *are* going to be interested in you."

"I can't tell them or you or anybody else anything," said Eva hastily. "The papers were just old letters— the wedding certificate, receipted bills, stuff her mother stuck away in drawers over the years and forgot. She would read it out loud to me sometimes:

'Pork chops, green pepper, loaf of bread, pound of coffee'—it came to eighty-five cents. And she would figure out what it cost to shop for the pound of pork chops, green pepper, loaf of bread, and coffee nowadays. I'm telling you, that Gladys was a weirdie."

"I don't see how anyone, no matter how weird, could spend all the time mulling over a handful of papers."

"It wasn't a handful—it was a small trunk or foot locker," said Eva. "Living with Gladys reminded me of entertaining a country cousin. Know what I mean? The talk about all the dead aunts and uncles. I think when her mother died, Gladys' clock stopped and began running backward."

The sound of the front-door chimes dropped abruptly into our midst.

"That'll be the police," James Holadare said unnecessarily.

He went to answer.

ELEVEN

It was squad-car cops first, and then a homicide detail headed by a Lieutenant Bert Hendryx, who questioned us separately and lengthily. Past ten o'clock, Kelly and I were turned loose to drive off in the station wagon with the dry snow pellets whisking across the car roof and glass.

"What was the telephone call all about?" I asked.

Kelly thought back. "I guess Holadare was trying to break the news gently and his mother broke in."

"What'd his mother say?"

"I'm trying to remember exactly, and I think her words were: 'They've found them?' "

"Found who?"

"I don't know, because Holadare said no, no, it was a dead man at the door. And that he was going to have to call the police."

"So she said—?"

"She said to let her know how it came out. Ken, who are they and them?"

"I don't know—"

"Or you're not telling. I'm only your wife, not the awfully attractive Miss Eva Shelton. You hardly took your eyes off her the whole evening."

"There wasn't any use looking at you for the answers." I thought awhile. "We can't spend our lives accusing each other of misbehaving with every Roy Elling and Eva Shelton who comes along," I said. "Let's cut it out, talk about something pleasant."

Kelly thought awhile, too. "The Holadares have a really beautiful house. What do you suppose it takes to buy a house like that?"

"Around forty thousand, but I imagine the Holadares got it thrown in with the oil painting and the breakfront."

"Forty thousand! Oh, I don't think so."

"The lot alone must have set them back ten thousand, maybe twelve."

"Then the house itself could be built on a lot in Milquevais for twenty-eight thousand or less," said Kelly. "A person could leave one of the bedrooms and a bath to be added in the future, and the basic house mightn't cost more than twenty-two five or even twenty thousand."

"A lot of cash."

"People don't pay cash; they swing it with a down payment and the rest like rent."

"We'll keep it in mind in case I write a best-seller. Or in case I collected the reward for turning in the murderer of Gladys Irvine."

"How much did you pay Senor What's-His-Name?" said Kelly.

"Hundred dollars."

"And sixteen hundred and the plane tickets. Do you realize in the last few days we've spent enough to make the down payment on a home of our own?"

Ahead loomed the Mother Goosey filling station.

I swung onto its concrete apron and braked short of the gas pumps.

"It's no use crying over spilled milk, and I have to phone Ed Horace—"

There was a booth inside the station building, and Ed Horace took the call at the Milquevais end. I told him what I'd been able to learn from Lieutenant Hendryx: "Riker seems to have been an asphyxiation victim like the Irvine girl—no marks of violence aside from a few minor bruises and contusions. It might not be carbon monoxide this time, though—Hendryx doesn't seem to think so, but he hasn't an autopsy report yet. The crazy part is that *rigor mortis* indicates he may have been killed in Milquevais and hauled all the way to Larksdale. Perhaps as a warning to others who might try to collect the reward?"

"Had Riker tried to collect the reward?" said Ed's flu-stuffed voice. "Walter Burch doesn't know about it, and Burch is the man to see about claiming the reward."

"Maybe the killer is sore at the Holadares for butting in. Leaving the body here could have been a way of paying them off by involving them in a police investigation and newspaper notoriety."

"I'm too sick a man to try and figure it all out, and I wish you'd hurry back here, Ken."

I promised to return to Milquevais at once.

It didn't work out that way, though, for as I crossed the filling station yard toward the station wagon, I heard a faint, smothered gasp:

"Help!"

My first thought was of Kelly. I found her seated quietly in the Chevie.

"Ken, I've been thinking— Maybe instead of jump-ing bail, I should go back to Mexico and stand trial."

Again came the choked cry for help.

"Listen!" I said. "You hear that?"

Kelly answered, "Yes, it's the radio in the car down the street. Some crook drama."

The filling station stood at the intersection of a main drag and a side street. Parked at the side-street curb, at a distance of ninety or a hundred feet, stood a coupe.

I walked toward it.

Up close, I saw that it had been parked long enough for the fine snow to have blanketed the street around the tires. There was no dash light burning, and no hum of radio.

"Hello, there?" I said.

A muffled sob answered. So did a flurry of queer bumping noises. Both seemed to come from the coupe's luggage compartment.

I circled to the rear of the machine and tried to lift the luggage hatch. It was locked. From within came incoherent sounds. I sprang to the side door and found no keys dangling from the dash.

On the run, I returned to the station wagon, and on the run returned with the steel spud. I thrust the chisel end under the hatch in an effort to break the lock. It was a noisy business that brought Kelly and a coverall-clad attendant from the station.

To the latter, I threw: "How long has this car been parked here?"

"I don't know—"

The lock came apart, and dropping the spud, I threw up the hatch. An inside bulb lighted. Crumpled crookedly in the luggage trunk lay Jessica Riker, looking for all the world like a grotesquely oversized doll that had been abandoned by a careless child.

I saw her face first, a patch of flesh blued by cold, streaked with tear tracks, framed in disordered tangles of dark hair. Off one cheek dripped a peel of adhesive tape that had originally covered her mouth. Her lips showed smears of the adhesive.

She gestured convulsively, poking out a blue-cold and dirty hand. From the wrist dangled a clutter of tape. The skirt had dropped from her doubled-up knees. Her thighs were goose-pimpled, her knees chafed and soiled. More tape was wound around her ankles.

I half-pulled and half-lifted Jessica Riker out of the trunk. Deadweight, she slumped and moaned in my arms. She was too heavy to carry, so I told Kelly to get our car.

The station attendant yammered something about calling a doctor, calling the cops.

"We'll take her to the cops."

We headed toward the Holadares', Kelly driving while I bundled the car robe around Mrs. Riker, supported her in the seat, and tried to find out what had happened.

She managed some answers through chattering teeth. "I was fixin' dinner. They sneak up behind me."

"Who?"

"I didun look aroun'. Jus' thought it was Ralph come in the house." Water ran out of the big woman's eyes and nose. She snuffled like a child too young to know how to blow its nose.

"They threw a sack over my head. It stunk. It was chloroform or ether or somethin'."

The robe twitched with the shaking of her big body. The robe smelled of anti-freeze.

"Then you saw no one?" I asked.

"I couldun. I passed out— When I come to, I was in the back of the movin' car an' tied han' and foot." There was light enough to watch her eyes rolling in tear-filled sockets. "I smelled the gas, and I thought to myself, 'I'm goin' to die like poor Gladys.' "

"You're all right now," said Kelly from the wheel.

Again I asked what else happened.

"Fin'ly the car stopped, the door slammed, they lef' me there—"

"Just *one* door slammed?"

"Yes, and after, while I rolled around, I found a tire iron. I held the tire iron between my knees and sawed and sawed and got my hands loose."

"And then?"

"I jus' lay there. I figured they was coming back. I was going to try to hit them with the tire iron. Until it got so cold I give up and begun hollerin' for help."

Kelly braked the station wagon. Mrs. Riker lifted her head and rolled her eyes.

"Where am I? What place is this?"

The place was the Holadare's split-level.

Lieutenant Hendryx had a background of police ambulance experience from his days in uniform. He knew the routine of treating drunks and jack-rolled victims and heart cases picked up freezing in slum doorways and city alleys.

His preoccupation with Mrs. Riker gave me the chance to slip Kelly the high sign. We drove back to the Mother Goosey, where a squad car had arrived and was checking over the coupe. The coupe belonged to Ralph Riker, and the tire iron in the luggage compartment was sticky with white gum from adhesive tape. The car keys could not be found.

I went into the station phone booth and long-distanced these developments to Ed Horace.

"My god!" said Ed. "Why'd they kill Ralph but leave his wife alive?"

"I don't know, but possibly the idea was to keep her out of circulation during the time needed to move Ralph's body from Milquevais to Larksdale."

"But why move him?"

"Gladys Irvine wasn't left lying where she died, either," I said. "There seems to be a compulsion to play Halloween pranks with the corpses."

I hung up and looked into the booth's telephone directory. A Mrs. Helen Holadare lived in Dupont South.

TWELVE

The house was a multi-chimneyed pile of Robber Baron-era architecture, built on a corner and looking down a side street at the frozen waste of Lake Harriet. The notion entered my mind that anyone living with this view conceived the idea of planting a corpse under ice. The notion took much of the force out of my suggestion to Kelly:

"Sweetheart, suppose you sit this one out in the car."

"Wait outside all by myself? Why should I?"

"I don't want you falling in love with a castle and worrying your head how we're to raise the down payment on one like it."

"Very funny," said Kelly, "but I don't intend to give anyone the chance of dropping a chloroformed sack over my head."

"You could lock the car, and there's even the shotgun in the back—"

"So you admit I'd be in danger!"

Kelly climbed out of the Chevie, and I gave up the argument. It didn't seem an argument worth winning, particularly if Helen Holadare refused to see callers at this hour.

We followed a curving walk into grounds too large to be called a yard, too small to be described as a park.

Enclosing hedges, shrubbery, and trees broke the wind, and the thin snowfall lay undisturbed except for a single set of footprints tracking up the walk ahead.

The house had brick bastion walls, ornamentally grated windows, and a fortress door. This door was opened by an aged mulatto man who'd one hand resting on the collar of the world's largest Weimaraner. Or maybe the dog was half-Weimaraner and half-wolf.

"My name's Svederup," I said rapidly, and added slowly and distinctly, "I've just come from James Holadare's, and it's of the utmost importance for me to see his mother immediately."

"Step inside," the mulatto said agreeably. Then, slowly and distinctly, he added, "Don't try to pat the Count. Don't put your hand into your pocket for a handkerchief or anything like that."

"He doesn't like handkerchiefs?" asked I.

"He don't like hands in pockets." The mulatto went away, leaving Kelly and me looking at each other, and the dog looking at us both.

"I think I'm going to sneeze," said Kelly weakly.

"Press your finger to your lip under your nose," I said. "The Count may be allergic to sneezes and other sudden noises."

We had three or four minutes to admire the dog's lovely silver-gray coat and liquid blue eyes before the mulatto returned.

"Mrs. Holadare will see you in the cardroom."

Off we went on a conducted tour up a hallway,

through several large and ill-lighted rooms, hunks
of the kind of statuary that spouts water in gardens,
vases almost big enough for a man to hide in, and
gilded frames surrounding gloomy oil paintings.

The cardroom proved to be a kind of alcove. It
contained a card table, not the folding kind—this
one was furniture. Mrs. Helen Holadare sat there
behind a layout of Idiot's Delight.

Mrs. Holadare was a woman of about sixty, with
silver-gray hair and liquid blue eyes. I don't know
what made me suspect she might be half-woman and
half-wolf.

"That will be all for the present, Jefferson," she
told the mulatto. "You may leave the Count with
me."

The mulatto retired, and the Weimaraner ghosted
to an opposite wall and lay down under a dark oil
painting of two New England-type old cronies playing checkers.

"My son sent you?" Helen Holadare asked. She
asked me, but her blue eyes appraised Kelly for reaction.

"No," I said. "I came on my own. It occurred to
me James couldn't keep you very well posted over
the phone, not with the house full of cops, and I
thought you might be interested in the latest bulletin from the crime front."

"But who are you two?"

"Will the Count object if I put my hand in my
pocket and produce the identification?"

"Please do."

I unbuttoned the topcoat and opened the wallet and displayed the proof that I was Kenneth Svederup of the Milquevais *Globe.* "And this is Mrs. Svederup. We just flew in from California tonight in time to be greeted by the arrival of Ralph Riker's body." I covered that and repeated Jessica Riker's account of the kidnaping. "Gladys Irvine lived with these people," I said, "and the natural inference is that Riker was killed because he dug up some clue. He didn't attempt to communicate with County Attorney Burch, though, so you see—"

"See? What am I supposed to see?"

I watched her studying me, and I felt the dog studying me, and therefore I pitched my voice pleasantly:

"Burch could pay only five thousand, and maybe Riker figured somebody else would raise the ante."

The Weimaraner wasn't fooled a bit, and let an answering growl slip from his throat.

Mrs. Holadare was smoother. She was also a little longer in answering. "Who would raise the ante, as you put it?" she said finally.

"Your son?" I suggested.

The dog got up on his four feet. Mrs. Holadare merely laughed.

"James couldn't begin to raise as much as five thousand in ready cash. He isn't a wealthy man, only a salaried employee of the Holadare Company. He's kept strapped supporting an extravagant wife, keeping up the payments on a costly motor car and a mink coat not to mention the bills for her clothing and what she spends in the beauty salons."

The Count settled down again, head between his paws. He must have decided Helen Holadare was enjoying the conversation, and that's what I decided, too.

"You don't approve of Midge?" I asked.

"I believe a woman should be a helpmeet, not a millstone around her husband's neck," said Helen Holadare."

Kelly spoke up. "But if he loves her and she loves him," she said.

The Weimaraner yawned.

"There's more to successful marriage than romantic love." Helen Holadare's blue eyes were less liquid; in fact, there were steely. "The family is an economic unit. It's function is property management, the bulding of an estate, getting ahead in the world. I'm quoting Aristotle, the sage of the ages, and modern-day divorce-court statistics bear him out. The moment married couples begin to fall behind financially, they also begin to fall apart matrimonially."

Kelly caught her breath and bit her lip.

"I was a helpmeet to my husband," Helen Holadare said. "Charles, at the time we married, worked as a radio repairman, spent his spare time inventing a static suppressor, had the dream he could sell the patent for a million dollars. In fact, he received a flat offer of a thousand. He would have sold out for that, but I insisted otherwise. I set him to work making the thing by hand in the garage, and I myself went from door to door selling the device. That's how the Holadare Company came into being."

Her words carried me back to La Jolla, to old H. H. Crossway bragging of the basement job press that acorned the Crossway newspaper chain. Only this time the story had a fresh twist.

"Okay, T-birds and mink cost money," I said, "but so does divorce cost money. Surely a court would award Midge substantial alimony, and to get rid of her you might have to make a hefty property settlement—"

Mrs. Holadare stared at me before replying. "I've always understood plaintiffs have to come into court with clean hands."

"Is that why you offered the five-thousand reward? In the hope of finding some dirt on Midge's hands?"

The dog stood up. So did Helen Holadare. "I'll walk to the door with you," she said.

Again, I decided against arguing. She had the dog on her side. Also, I wasn't sure how the Weimaraner would react to the suggestion that James Holadare might have killed Ralph Riker because Ralph had something on Midge, perhaps had tried to blackmail her. After all, I didn't *know* Riker's body had been on the doorstep. The corpse could have been parked around the corner of the split-level house.

But then who'd rung the door chimes?

Kelly and I made the return trek to the station wagon. We drove off down the street, and Kelly said,

"Ken, in a way she's right. Money *is* important. If we'd gained a couple of thousand dollars instead of losing it, we wouldn't be snapping at each other like this."

At the block's end, I U-turned the Chevie. "You've only heard the one side of it," I said. "'*She* claims she was a helpmeet. Charles Holadare disappeared thirty years ago. He may have given the ball and chain the slip—a lot of guys do."

I drove across the street and braked a few rods away from the Robber Baron roost. I switched off the lights and killed the motor.

"So my mind's made up what to do," said Kelly. "Yeah?"

"I'm going to be a helpmeet. When we get back to Milquevais, I'm going out and find myself a job."

I didn't answer. My gaze was fixed on the fortress front door. It opened, and Dirk Lebijohn came out of it, buttoning up his trenchcoat.

THIRTEEN

Kelly, more than half asleep in the seat beside me, less than half woke as the front wheels bumped against the platform edge. "Home?" she asked.

"Indian Rock," I explained.

Kelly drowsed off. I got up and crossed the brick platform and entered the Indian Rock railroad station. It was bigger than the Wydota one and had a modern oil burner instead of an antique coal-burning stove.

According to the bulletin board, the local, which left Milquevais at nine-thirty and passed through Wydota at ten-two reached Indian Rock at ten forty-one. Gladys Irvine would have had to wait until eleven-four to catch the main line limited into Minneapolis. On the return trip, she would have gotten into Indian Rock at eight forty-eight and boarded the branch line at ten fifty-two to arrive in Milquevais at midnight.

It gave me food for thought as I drove on out of Indian Rock on Highway 8, against thin fleeting snowflakes diagonaling into the headlight beam. Fence, telephone, and REA poles marched in parade. The car light caught jewel flashes from the small animal eyes of cottontails and weasels and stray cats.

The striped back of a skunk darted across the road. The red brush of a fox disappeared into a weed-thicket on a bank of earth left by a drag-line ditching outfit.

The prairie scenery acted like a tonic to common sense. Country crime, I mused, is usually as plain as country cooking. The ingredients are home-grown, served without exotic French sauces. Gladys Irvine sitting for two hours between trains at Indian Rock violated common sense. She could have caught a bus out of Minneapolis; the bus would have landed her in Milquevais in two hours.

After a while, the tires bumped over the tracks again to another station platform.

"Home?" mumbled Kelly.

"Wydota," I explained.

"I thought you said Indian Rock."

She fell asleep. I went into the Wydota station waiting room, banged on the ticket window, and called Leslie Jopperman's name.

Les came down from upstairs and let me into the ticket office. The light over the telegraph key disclosed that he wore a blue flannel robe over a peppermint-striped nightshirt, that his kewpie face looked strangely chapped, that he had Band-Aids in the palms of both hands.

"Hi, podner," I said. "We are podners, aren't we?"

"You make that remark sound invidious," said Les.

"My thoughts are invidious, Leslie. I'm wonder-

ing how the hell you happened along to find me unconscious in the *Globe* parking lot."

"Oh, that." He saw me looking at his palms. He
closed his hands. "It's very simple, Kenny. I thought
if we were going into the *Bloody Murder Magazine*
contest, we ought to have a written agreement about
dividing the money if we won any."

"And in the excitement you forgot what you came
for?"

"You were hurt, and I decided to skip it until you
felt better."

I didn't think so. He had learned I was leaving
for the West Coast, that he was going to do the leg-
work, that he could probably enter the contest without my help. Did he still figure it that way.

"I'm feeling fine now," I said. "Are we still podners?"

Leslie turned to the desk, made a sandwich of
telegraph flimsies and carbon paper, and with indelible pencil rapidly scribbled and signed. I scanned
the sandwich. It was a straightforward, explicit, and
uncompromising contract to go fifty-fifty on the magazine contest. No mention in it of the five thousand
dollar reward.

I said, "It's a limited podnership, huh? You figure
you need my help enough to cut me in on the *Bloody
Murder* deal, but at the same time you hope to glom
onto the Holadare reward all by yourself."

Les's chapped face reddened with a blush.

"It's okay by me, Les. Frankly, I prefer it this
way."

I signed, tore off the original, and returned the indelible pencil and carbon copy. At the moment, Les Jopperman bore less-than-usual resemblance to a kewpie doll; he looked like a blazed-eyed carp out of water.

"Now that's out of the way," I continued, "I can tell you I've been doing a little legwork, and it may interest you to know Ralph Riker was killed to-night."

Leslie listened intently to my account of Riker's body turning up at the James Holadare home, and of my finding Mrs. Riker locked up in the luggage compartment of the Riker car. He frowned, passed his hand over his scalp, pushed his slippered feet into a scuffling to-and-fro prowling of the ticket-office floor.

"Maybe Harvey Staples killed the guy," he offered finally.

"Why would Harvey?"

"Revenge. Riker supplied Earl Bowers with the tip that led to Staples being nabbed on the muskrat-trapping rap."

"I didn't know that."

"You can take my word for it. Bowers naturally noticed the Oak Lake rat houses had been chopped into. He came in here and asked me who was shipping furs out of Wydota. I gave him Riker's name, and Riker admitted to buying over a hundred skins from Harvey Staples."

"Well?"

Les Jopperman allowed his features to light up

with a small-lipped smile. "The Bowers' baby telegram was a hoax," he said. "It induced Staples, who
was right there in the fishing crew, to think the game
warden was taking off for the Cities. Harvey felt
safe in resuming his trapping for a day or so, and was
himself trapped with his arm up to the shoulder in a
muskrat house. But it couldn't have happened if
Riker had tipped Harvey off that Bowers was laying
for him."

Up to a point, it sounded plausible. Violence in
Milquevais County frequently stems from just such
petty stuff.

"I understood Ralph Riker put up Staples' bail,
though," said I.

"Well, isn't that elementary, Kenny? Riker would
naturally pose as a friend, try to keep Staples from
guessing who did the squealing."

"Yes, but why'd Staples haul the body to Larksdale?"

Les shrugged. "Harvey has the cunning it takes to
outwit wild animals. He'd be smart enough to cover
his own tracks by diverting the suspicion to some
other quarter."

I asked quietly, "You don't think Staples also killed
Gladys Irvine, do you?"

Les's eyelids pulled down like window blinds,
making his face as stolid as a blank wall.

"I can't prove who killed Gladys, of course."

"You've ideas, though. What was the libelous story
you wrote that Ed Horace refused to print?"

He had ideas, all right, and now his face betrayed

an industrious effort to sort through these ideas and sort out the one least likely to lead me closer to the five thousand payoff.

"Never mind, Les. I can always ask Ed and get the straight of it from him," I said.

"Then ask him and to hell with you!"

FOURTEEN

Waking up the next morning, I blinked a 10-A.M. sunbeam out of my eyes. The sunbeam had strayed in around the slightly frayed edge of a window blind. I turned my head the other way, gazed at the adjacent and empty twin bed, and concluded that Kelly would be calling me to breakfast any minute.

I rolled out, ran up the blind, and faced a day so warm and sunny that already water was dripping off the eaves.

Detouring the suitcases near the doorway, I made for the bathroom. It was not a carpeted bathroom; it lacked a shower stall; the towel rack was apt to come off with a hastily grabbed towel. I cleaned up and shaved, momentarily expecting the breakfast call.

I returned to the bedroom; I got dressed; I wandered out through the living room. It was not in the same class with the James Holadares' living room. It had mopboards, for one thing. They used to build mopboards around the base of rooms to keep the scrub water from splashing on the wallpaper. The furniture matched the mopboards: we had decided not to buy new pieces that might not fit into a new house when we got around to affording a new house.

This morning our living room depressed me.

So did the kitchen. It was a linoleum-floored kitchen equipped with hot and cold running water at the cast-iron sink, a gas stove fed from a tank outside the house, and drop-cord bulbs. From the double-socket over the kitchen table dripped a cord connected to the toaster.

"Kelly?" I said.

She wasn't here, and didn't answer, and that depressed me, too. Until I realized there'd been no shopping done in over a week. Kelly had probably gone out for bread and milk, things like that.

I suddenly noticed the note stuck in the toaster. *Have gone job hunting,* it said.

She'd had a cup of coffee before leaving. The drip pot stood on the gas stove. It was cold. I lighted the flame under it, then stepped out to the front porch and picked up the morning's *Globe.*

The news was no fresher than the warmed-over coffee. I found myself blankly staring at the one and untastingly swallowing the other. In truth, I had not really expected Kelly to rush out in search of a job.

Somehow the whole deal gave me the Tijuana blues—the same trapped and helpless sensation of being life's pushed-around pawn.

I heard the station wagon stop outside. Its door slammed. A sound of running feet came up the walk and across the porch.

Kelly flung open the front door and a moment later appeared in the kitchen doorway. She stared at me hazily out of tear-flooded eyes. Then she whirled and went the other way, toward the bedroom.

I caught up with her just before she could slam the bedroom door in my face.

We had words:

"What happened?" I said.

"Nothing!" she said.

"You're crying!"

"I'm not, and will you kindly please mind your own darned business?"

"What are you crying for?"

"I'm not crying. I'm mad. I've never been so damned mad or so *humiliated* in my life."

"What happened?"

"Oh, I suppose I might as well tell you."

We returned to the kitchen, and over the re-warmed coffee, Kelly explained she had started her employment hunt by paying a call at the library "—because Florrie Schultz knows the town inside out, and always has, and I assumed she'd be the best one to advise me where to start looking for a job."

Florrie, Kelly went on to say, had recommended starting at the Farmers Cooperative Creamery; because, so far as Florrie knew, nothing had been done about replacing Gladys Irvine. Olin Wolff had served so many years on the Library Board that undoubtedly a note from Florrie would induce him to accept Kelly's advance application. Even though the job mightn't be filled for a few more weeks.

"So I drove out there," said Kelly, "and gave Mr. Wolff Florrie's note, which he didn't even bother to read. He went away and about ten minutes later came back with a form for me to fill out—a form as long as my arm, with spaces for when and where I was born, where educated, marital status, previous occupational experience, three local references, and so on and so on. I spent fully three-quarters of an hour filling it all in, and after all that, Mr. Wolff said he'd been thinking it all over and as treasurer he did not feel he could take a chance on employing a person under indictment on gambling charges."

"He turned you down because of your police record?"

"I didn't mind that," said Kelly. "It's rather exciting to be cast as the Milquevais gambling moll. What I resented was being made to fill out that infernal form, every last detail about myself, when all the time he knew he'd turn me down."

She was giving me ideas.

"I'm sure Olin Wolff didn't mean to hurt your feelings. He's under the gun, facing an annual meeting when he's got to explain to a bunch of sorehead farmers how over twenty-five hundred dollars of their money could vanish from under his nose. In fact, he's peering into both tubes of a double-barrel gun."

"What do you mean?"

"It's just an old sporting expression."

I kissed Kelly, rushed to the Chevie, and drove through the bright sunny forenoon to the Co-op plant. I parked among slush-spattered cars, pushed through the glass-slab doors, and climbed the stairs.

The treasurer's office lay deserted except for the old man sitting in the zebra-stripe of his Venetian-blinded cubicle. He turned his head at the sound of my footfalls on the cork-tiled floor. I threw him a handwave. He ignored it and swung his head back to a fistful of papers.

"Mr. Wolff," I said.

He put down the papers. "Oh, hullo, Ken. Glad to see you're back. Mrs. Svederup was in this morning, and I've been thinking since, maybe there's an opening in some other department. It didn't occur to me at the time—I'm up to my ears. Swedenborg went to the Cities to bring Mrs. Riker home. I understand she collapsed completely on being told of Ralph's death."

All of this in a garrulous rush of words from under the white mustache.

"Ralph's who I dropped in to see you about, Mr. Wolff. I have to write up the obituary for the paper, and it occurred to me you might still have the job application form he filled out."

"Let's have a look in the personnel files." Olin Wolff, walking tiredly, led the way to the rear of the business office. He stopped in front of a row of green metal cases, snapped his fingers, and grumbled, "Blamed if I didn't leave my reading specs back on the desk. Suppose you look it up—as I told you, I'm up to my ears."

"Sure, don't let me keep you from the salt mine."

I rolled out the R drawer and fished into Ralph Riker's folder. I found duplicate records on his income-tax withholdings (he'd been earning $125 a week on his truck), records of Blue Cross deductions (he'd never been sick a day), and back of everything else his job application.

Riker, according to this, had been born 3 September 1925 in Laguna County, Oregon; had graduated from the Trier Township High School; had gone into the Navy and then worked three years in the Merchant Marine. His job record included a stretch in a logging camp, a year with a van and storage company in Portland, another year on a bread route in St. Louis, then two years as a milkman in St. Paul. He'd come to Milquevais in 1955, worked six months with the Prairie States Fuel & Refrigeration Company, after which he'd switched to the Co-op. His local references were Sam Flack, the Prairie States manager; T. O. Heggland, owner of the local bowling alley; and the Milquevais First National.

I returned to the doorway of Olin Wolff's cubicle. Staring through his reading specs at the sheaf of papers, he said, "Come on in, sit down, have a cigar. I'll be through in a minute."

I came in, sat down, and helped myself to a cigar. I peeled the band from the cigar, and laid that on the desk. Next I peeled a strip of wrapper leaf off the cigar and placed that on the desk.

"There was nothing to indicate whether Ralph's parents are still living," I said.

Olin Wolff put down the papers, took off the glasses, and put them down on top of the papers.

I unwound another leaf of wrapper from the cigar. "Or whether he was survived by any brothers or sisters."

"Mrs. Riker would probably know about the family connections," Olin Wolff said.

I went on peeling the cigar and piling up the shreds on the desk. Nothing in the old man's face expressed any surprise.

I said, "How long have you been practically blind, Mr. Wolff?"

Still the old man's face didn't change very much. It was a face he'd worn a long time.

"I'm not blind, Ken. Of course, my eyes aren't what they used to be when it comes to the fine print."

"And when it comes to signing the checks?"

Suddenly the zebra stripes of sun and shadow no longer looked like zebra stripes. The effect was of Olin Wolff peering toward me through an arrangement of bars.

"I went to Rochester, and the docs there gave me some drops that help quite a bit—"

"Enough so you can see me sitting here, Mr. Wolff?"

"Sure, I can see you."

"But not the cigar?"

Olin Wolff did a funny thing. He made a fist of his right hand, raised the fist to his eye, and squinted at me through the tiny telescope made by his bunched fingers.

"I should have remembered you don't smoke them, Ken."

"I'm sorry, but I had to pull it on you."

"You don't have to be sorry for me. The docs expect to save about eighty per cent of my vision, but it'll take a series of operations. I just figured I could stick it out until the annual meeting and then retire on my pension."

"I know, you couldn't quit before the annual meeting. If it got out you're through, there'd be six to eight fellows gunning for the treasurer's job, and Swede wouldn't have a prayer."

"A man owes something to his own son."

"Especially a son who's been carrying the workload of signing your name to the checks," I said.

At the Prairie States I found Sam Flack in the warehouse knocking the crating off a shipment of tanks of bottled gas. There were No Smoking signs all over the place, and Sam worked over a tobacco cud as he talked.

"Yup, I gave Ralph the reference. Glad to. He drove one of our trucks awhile, and he was a good man, a hustler. Hated to see him go, but the Co-op pays salary, and with us it's a commission deal."

"Do you know if he left surviving parents, brothers, or sisters?"

"I don't recall he ever mentioned. Of course, it's been years. I haven't seen Ralph to talk to since he left. Well, he dropped in a month or so ago and bought some dry ice."

"What'd he want of dry ice?"

"Bum motor in the deep freeze; he was going to stick the dry ice in until he got around to working on the motor. Ralph was a saving guy when it came to odd jobs."

At the First National Bank, I went into a huddle with Eldon Rickert. Rickert was the bank's president, an old-fashioned bank president of the silver-maned and pince-nez type. He was at first fairly frosty: "I imagine you knew when a man dies his bank account is sealed pending release by the tax assessment and probate authorities. You've been around the court-house long enough to realize I can't open the bank's records to your inspection."

"Okay, Mr. Rickert. But do you remember writing a letter of reference to the Co-op on Riker's behalf?"

"No, I don't. I doubt if I would have written a let-ter. The chances are I picked up the phone and told them that Riker opened an account of around thirty-five hundred dollars when he first came to Milque-vais. He built up the account by means of regular and substantial deposits."

"A saving man."

"He was hard-working and thrifty. Most young fellows nowadays are either in debt or operating on such a slender financial margin that they're wiped out by the first emergency."

I went into the North Star Bowling Alleys and ordered a noonday burger and coffee from T. O. Heggland, proprietor. T.O. was a big, bald man wearing a tee shirt that left bare his bowling-ball-sized biceps.

"Helluva thing happened to Ralph," said he. "Ralph was a guy you couldn't say a word against."

I waited. People who can't say a word-against always do, and generally in the next breath.

"He had a sense of humor," T.O. divulged. "Always coming in here and kidding me about the money I made. Kidding how someday he'd buy me out—what would I take for a down payment. Certain people took that kind of talk serious, but actually Ralph was just kidding."

"Maybe you should have taken him up on it, T.O."

"Nah, I just ribbed him back. For instant, he'd say how about twelve grand on the barrelhead, and I'd say not a nickel less than fifteen thou." T. O. Heggland laughed.

"Deadpan?" I said.

"What?"

"I imagine the humor was in the straight-faced way he said it."

"Oh, sure. Anyway, you couldn't say a truthful word against the guy. Except now and then he'd hit the bottle a little hard."

"Whose bottle?"

T. O. Heggland laughed again. "Well, I hafta admit he done a certain amount of freeloading. We threw a little party out at my house New Year's, and by 2 A.M. Ralph was so plastered he hadda be carried to the car."

"Maybe he was kidding," I said.

Ed Horace usually appeared at the *Globe* office around noon. I found him behind his desk, sucking a fever thermometer instead of the usual pipestem.

The bifocals magnified the flu-reddened eyes he raised from the forenoon mail.

"Damn it, Ken," Ed said, trickling the words around the thermometer, "here's a letter from the Old Man instructing me to withhold fifteen bucks a week from your pay. What's it all about?"

"The Old Man decided to turn over a new leaf, and I am under it."

Ed Horace removed and read the thermometer. "A hundred and two. I'm living on aspirin and antibiotics, got a headache the size of a bushel basket. For God's sake, talk sense."

"It's just a joke I picked up while trying to dig up an obit on Ralph Riker," I said. "By the way, what was the trouble between you and Les Jopperman?"

Ed played the thermometer bulb across his lower teeth.

"Funny you mentioning Ralph, because that was the trouble. Jopperman dug up a story to the effect that last December Ralph was dickering to buy out Heggland's bowling alley. He's supposed to have offered twelve thousand down and the balance at six per cent, but T.O. held out for fifteen thousand cash and seven per cent."

"Well?"

"You can add and subtract. Ralph needed an additional $3000 just at the time $2580 disappeared from the Co-op and Gladys Irvine got murdered. I should print such a thing and get the *Globe* sued for a million dollars?"

"So you threw it in the wastebasket?"

"No, I turned it over to Walter Burch," said Ed. "How you are making out with the obit?"

"I haven't found yet whether Ralph left any survivors other than Jessica, but I'm still trying."

Still trying, I headed the Chevie down the main drag and across the Mud Hen tracks, where a left turn put me on Superior. Superior followed the tracks, a street too close to the noise and smoke of passing freights to be anything choice residentially.

The 1800 block took me practically to the edge of open country. It had been open country when the house was built—a big, two-story, mustard-colored house sitting behind rows of apple and plum trees and in front of a pair of couching unpainted sheds. Everything about the layout indicated the retirement Shrangri-La of a farmer who had moved close to town around 1910 with the idea of raising his fruit, milking a cow, tending a flock of hens and hoeing a garden.

The farmer's name had been Axel A. Axelson. The name was still on the rural-style mailbox on the fence post in front of the property. The flag was up. The blinds in the house windows were down.

I braked at the box and looked into it. The mail consisted of a Clerk of Court's envelope addressed to Ralph Riker, a mail-order health-foods ad addressed to Gladys Irvine, and a letter that had been addressed to Babe Riker in St. Louis, Missouri, marked *Please Forward—Addressee Unknown—Return to Sender*. The sender being J. Riker, who'd mailed it from Milquevais on 27 January.

It's against Federal law to open other people's mail.
I propped this envelope on the mailbox door, rested
the Graphic on the car window, and took its picture.

Then I drove on and at the block's end came to
Terminal Avenue. Terminal dipped through an underpass beneath the tracks and ran on a third of a
mile to the plate glass and glass brick of the Farmers
Cooperative Creamery.

Much closer, only a hundred feet away, sat the plate
glass, chrome, and white paint of a T-bird.

I turned the other way on Terminal, drove a dozen
rods, and jumped out to climb the woven-wire fence
enclosing the plum and apple orchard. A hike
through the spongy snow under the trees brought me
to a second fence, with a gate into the Rikers' backyard. The opened doors of the nearest shed showed
the interior of an empty dirt-floored garage.

I advanced toward the silent, blind-drawn house.
It had an enclosed rear porch. The porch door was
locked.

Along the side of the building were a pair of Prairie
States LP gas tanks and a cellar door—the kind you
slid down as a kid if you were a kid in a town like
Milquevais. I raised this door and went down
wooden steps to a landing and a second, upright door.

This one's lock had been broken. Maybe by Sheriff Popke last night.

I entered a basement, more or less lighted by sunlight from sashes in the house foundations. It was a
cement-floored basement with cement-block walls. It
contained a coal-burning furnace that'd been con-

verted to oil, an oil-storage tank, a washing machine and dryer unit, a former butcher's ice chest that'd been converted to an electrical deep freeze. I looked longer at a faded blue chenille rug spread on the floor under a horizontal bar suspended from the house timbers. Beyond the rug and against the wall stood a row of Indian clubs. I picked up a club and carried it up the inside stairs into the kitchen.

It was a hot-and-cold-running-water kitchen, with mopboards. On the stove I observed a skillet of corned-beef hash, a cooking pot containing green peas, and a coffee percolator. An emptied can with a garden-peas label sat on the sink.

The kitchen opened into a dining room with a table set for two, a basket of stale sliced bread as its centerpiece. The dining room gave into a living room, which in turn led me to a front hallway with stairs to the second floor.

Down the stairs came sounds like rats making nests of papers.

Taking a tight grip on the Indian club's neck, I tiptoed up the stairs and along the upper hallway. The rat rustlings guided me to an open bedroom doorway.

Inside was a bed littered with the contents of a bureau drawer, the bureau drawer itself, and Dirk Lebijohn pawing through the papers and tossing them back into the bureau drawer. He had his back to me, but I recognized the trenchcoat.

I dropped the Indian club.

He froze, unfroze, plunged his right hand into the

slash pocket and whirled, pointing the pocket at me.

"Stick 'em up!" Lebijohn said. His sandy face changed. "Oh, it's you." Gloom ran down his face like wax drippings on a candle.

"What are you up to?" I said.

"I have as much right as you. I have *more* right, morally. What would you do with five thousand if you had it, Svederup?"

His mind was as full of surprises as a modernistic painting. But I'm logical about these things: "It won't be five thousand after Uncle Sam takes his bite," I pointed out.

"You would think of that, you with your middle-class materialistic outlook. You'd pay the income tax, then blow yourself to a bigger car and a thinner television. The money would change nothing; the only effect would be to make you more than ever the all-American consumer." His expression grew lofty. "Do you realize five thousand would finance a year's study in Paris and Italy for me? Don't you know in your heart your petty bourgeois ambitions are inferior to my creative dedication? I deserve the reward and you don't."

Listening, I cringed slightly. It's part of the small-town ethos to feel humble in the presence of Art and Culture. It seemed to me Florrie Schultz would be on this guy's side.

I said, "It happens I'm at work on an unfinished novel myself."

He laughed. "Then why don't you quit your lousy job and write your book? You don't have to compromise. I don't compromise. Look at me. I cut my own hair. I buy my clothes at church white-elephant bazaars. I refuse to prostitute my talent."

"Which talent? The one for hypnotism?"

"Hypnotism serves my art, too," said Dirk Lebi-john. "An artist needs models. Models cost money. They are unable to hold their poses without frequent rest periods. Hypnotized persons are able to remain practically rigid indefinitely. I took up mesmerism to put the models into light trances so my inspiration wouldn't be interrupted by the frequent rest periods."

Questioning him reminded me of trying to flood out a gopher by pouring pails of water down the gopher hole. The gopher always has another hole, an escape hatch.

"I thought you sold your pictures and went around with your pockets full of fifty-dollar bills," I said. "Did Midge Holadare slip you a thousand bucks during a light hypnotic trance?"

"I'm not going to help you buy the big fat car and the new thin television."

"Why'd you go to Helen Holadare's home last night?"

"Same answer."

He seemed to be inviting suspicion, perhaps in the hope of distracting me from the real issue. I stepped to the bed and looked down at the litter. I saw a paid and receipted dry-cleaning bill made out to Mrs. Ralph Riker, coupons worth ten cents on the purchase of various detergents and cake mixes, a letter from a Christmas card manufacturer promising door to door profits and beginning: *Dear Mrs. Riker.*

I said, "What's so interesting about Jessica Riker's stuff?"

Lebijohn readily volunteered, "I was hoping to find something of Gladys Irvine's the authorities might have overlooked. It seemed while I was here I might as well have a general look around. The Rikers might be concealing information. They're after the reward money, too."

All this time his hand stayed rooted in the trench-coat.

"Find anything?" I asked.

"Not a thing yet."

"Besides the fist, what's in your pocket?"

If looks could kill, I would have died on the spot—of the stake torture, with drawing and quartering thrown in for good measure.

But a gopher can't kill; it can only bolt for the nearest hole. Lebijohn bolted for the door. I thrust forth a foot. He fell over it with a crash that must have shook the horizontal bar in the basement.

I stooped and searched his pocket. It contained a packet of bank passbooks held together by a rubber band.

I examined them.

The first, shot as full of cancellation holes as Swiss cheese, was a St. Paul Mechanics & Drover's passbook that'd been issued to Jessica Clinton—Jessica Riker's maiden name. The account had been built up to thirty-five hundred odd dollars when closed out in mid-May of 1955.

The other books, all from the Milquevais First National, were all in Ralph Riker's name. It did not surprise me to discover that Ralph's original deposit of thirty-five hundred had been made just one week after Jessica withdrew *her* money from the Mechanics & Drovers.

Up to that time, Ralph had been a rolling stone; thereafter the moss accumulated rapidly, at first in forty- and fifty-dollar weekly deposits, later at a ninety- to hundred-dollar clip. Leafing the pages, I spotted but one withdrawal: on March 1, twelve hundred dollars had been taken out of the account. Even so, the final entry brought the total of deposits and interest to $12,789.23.

Only the latest book, of course, was current. Why had Jessica and Ralph hung onto the others? Why did Dirk Lebijohn think it worthwhile to pocket the lot?

I asked him.

He was on his feet again, scowling and nibbling at his lower lip.

"It could be where the Co-op's money went," Lebijohn said. "Maybe Mrs. Riker has been stealing from the vault all along. My theory is that Gladys became suspicious and the Rikers killed her. They not only killed her; they framed it to make people think Gladys was the thief."

I shook my head.

"What's wrong?" Lebijohn asked.

"Two things. Ralph was earning $125 a week, and Jessica probably $75 more, plus, I imagine, Gladys paid $25 for her room and board. The Rikers had an income of around $1000 a month." It seemed to me Helen Holadare would have admired them. H. H. Crossway, too. The Rikers were an economic unit, forging rapidly ahead in the world.

"They could easily have honestly saved every cent of the money," I continued. "Besides, you don't really think these passbooks solve Gladys' murder. The fact you offered me the theory proves you know it can never be traded in on the reward. That means you have other information and a different theory up your sleeve."

He paled so visibly that I wondered what I'd said that struck the sensitive nerve.

"You're in cahoots with Midge Holadare, aren't you?" I said. "She either brought you here, or she let you use her car—"

He interrupted: "Shut up. Listen."

I listened—to the sound of an idling motor somewhere out in front of the house. There came a tiny rasp and then a tinny bang—the opening and closing of the mailbox.

Lebijohn's breath hissed with the effort of lurching toward the blind-drawn window.

"Stay way from that," I said. "Maybe it's the carrier. And if anyone's coming in, fiddling with the blind won't stop them."

The tone of the motor deepened, and in low gear pulled closer to the house. It idled again, and died away. A car door slammed. A second slam echoed the first.

"Trapped," Dirk Lebijohn said. He wasn't a brave man; he was a dangerously frightened one.

Footfalls came around to the front of the house. They stomped, knocking off the slush. In another moment, voices came clearly up the stairs.

A woman's first: "I'm all in. I just want to hit the hay and sleep for a week."

And a man gruffed, "You have to talk to Walter Burch. You have to."

"I'm going up to the room and lie down a while first."

In a panting whisper, Dirk Lebijohn suggested, "Jump out the window—"

He would have risked breaking a leg to beat the risk of being arrested for housebreaking. What would he have risked to beat a murder rap?

I said, "I'll go down and shoo them into the kitchen, and you can sneak out the front way. Park in the lot behind the *Globe* building and wait for me there."

The pair were still arguing in the lower hallway.

"I already told the police everything I know ten times over," the woman said.

"They were city police. You were kidnaped in Milquevais County. Ralph was killed in Milquevais County. You have to go to Burch, or he and Popke will come after you."

I'd reached the head of the stairs. I gazed down on Jessica Riker, who had a foot on the lowermost step and a hand on the newel post. Her other arm was being restrained at the elbow by Swede Wolff.

They broke off the argument to stare up at me.

"Mr. Svederup," said Jessica, "what are you doing in my house?"

Her expression struck me as one of dark and sullen savagery.

Wolff, too, looked ugly, as if something had bestirred a hidden vitality, made more of him than the usual, languid replica of his father.

I came down the stairs. "I've been going through your things"—it's best at times to make out the worst case against yourself, and it seemed a fair gamble she wouldn't be eager to call in Willie Popke. I let the trial balloon float for a few seconds— "trying to find the materials I need to write your husband's obituary."

"I'm pooped," said Jessica Riker, and now she looked it. "Can't you come back later?"

"I have other work piled up, and now I'm here— There's a coffeepot on the stove, and couldn't I ask you a few questions over a cup of coffee?"

Swede finger-combed his yellow mustache. "Treat the newspaper right, Jessie, and the newspaper will treat you right."

Mrs. Riker turned and moved heavy-footed across the hall, the living room, the dining room, into the kitchen. Swede trailed her, and I tagged him, taking the time to close the doors.

It brought me last into the kitchen, just as Mrs. Riker picked up and shook the percolator and said in a thickly querulous voice, "Why, it's empty. Now who could have drunk all the coffee?"

I seemed to hear a clue drop and bounce, and seemed to see Swede Wolff trying to field it on the bounce. "Sheriff Popke was here investigating last night. He could've helped himself."

"That's so. I been half-killed, hauled and frozen in the back of the car till I can't think straight." Jessica rinsed the percolator at the sink, reloaded it at the kitchen cabinet, put it onto the burner. She dropped into a chair behind a formica-topped table, put her elbows on the table, all these movements suggesting that the bones in her big strong body had turned into lead.

Across the table I sat down with pencil and a folded sheet of copypaper. I asked when Ralph was born, and where. She gave the answers. I asked about surviving parents, brothers, or sisters.

"Ralph was an orphan—no close relatives at all."

"Then, as his widow, you will inherit the whole estate?"

In the subdued light of the blind-drawn kitchen Jessica Riker's face assumed the apearance of a white-floured bun dotted by two raisin eyes.

"I don't expect to inherit a dime," she said.

Was she just saying it because so often the sole benificiary is the number-one suspect? I had a feeling of more than that. Indeed, I had a feeling the house was floating off its foundations and going swimming down a dark flooded river.

"You don't expect a dime?" The bankbooks were now in my pocket. I took them out, sorted them, and flipped pages. "Surely you knew Ralph had twelve thousand and some seven hundred in the First National?" She had known their combined salaries and what it had cost them to live.

All the same, she hesitated.

Swede Wolff moved behind her chair and placed a hand on her shoulder. "You're going to have to tell Mr. Burch, and it will be in the paper, anyway."

Jessica said dully, "The money won't come to me. It'll go to Ralph's wife."

"You mean you're not—"

"No, I'm not."

I foresaw one of the damnedest obituaries ever to appear in the *Globe*.

"When did you find out?" I said.

"When I first started going with Ralph, he told me frankly he wasn't in a position to marry. He already had a wife down in St. Looie that he had walked out on. She wouldn't give him a divorce, not unless he bought her off."

"Did you give him thirty-five hundred to buy her off?"

"Yes, and he went down to St. Looie. But it wasn't enough. She put the bee on him for five thousand."

"*He* went to St. Louis? You weren't along?"

"He said Babe would be that much tougher to handle if she knew about me."

"Then you didn't meet her personally?"

"No, I never, but Ralph showed me her snapshot, and if God ever made a chippy, she was it."

"And Ralph, instead of returning the thirty-five

hundred to you, stuck it in the bank under his own name?"

Over on the stove, the percolator threw up its first bubble of water.

"We decided to pool our savings," Jessica said. "We hoped by both working and saving we could have the five thousand in a year. We figured we could get by cheaper and save faster living together."

I wondered what Helen Holadare and Old Man Crossway would have thought.

What Swede Wolff thought, he said: "Let him who is without sin cast the first stone." He stood behind Jessica's chair in an attitude of bowed-head and lowered-eyelids sympathy.

"And when your savings reached the five thousand goal?" I asked.

"It didn't seem right to throw the hard-earned money away on a chippy like Babe. If we had offered her the five thousand, she probably would've held out for ten. Then there was the chance she would fall for some other man and want to remarry herself and get the divorce. She might drop dead, as far as that went."

She might never have existed, as far as that went. I reserved judgment, and asked, "Then you never at any time paid Babe any money?"

"No, we never did."

"I notice here a withdrawal of twelve hundred dollars last March first."

Jessica reddened and twined and untwined her fingers.

"Well, you know Ralph always had the idea of going into business, and to do it he needed capital."

"The bowling-alley business?"

"That's right. Heggland wanted fifteen thousand down payment, and we didn't have it. Ralph heard of eighty acres he could cash-rent for twelve hundred and that's what he did. He figured he'd put the land into corn and make an extra three or four thousand."

Her redness of face persisted. What was the matter?

"Of course, working on the milk route, he had to do the farming by moonlight," she explained. "He rented a tractor and tools from the neighbors on holidays and Sundays. I'm ashamed to say he broke the Lord's commandment by laboring on the Sabbath."

It seemed to me several other commandments had been broken, but again I reserved judgment.

"The better the day, the better the deed," said Swede Wolff, looking up at the ceiling.

"Well, I don't know. The Lord sent the early snow before Ralph could reap the harvest."

In my memory, a cock pheasant rocketed in front of a fender and a jack rabbit bounded along an aisle of unpicked cornstalks. "The eighty acres didn't happen to be on the west shore of Oak Lake?" I said.

"That's the place," said Jessica.

Only a brief silence ensued before Swede Wolff spoke up. "You're making too much of it, Jessie," said he. "The snow fell on the just and the unjust alike, and God didn't send the October blizzard as a special punishment for Ralph."

Besides, the crop, or most of it, could be harvested when the snow melted. Say it ran fifty bushels to the acre, and deducting the expenses of picking and shelling and hauling to market, there'd be another three thousand for Babe to inherit.

"Do you still have Babe's snapshot?" I said.

"It might be around—" Jessica sounded unsure.

"It'd be a good idea to have it when you tell this story to Walter Burch."

Jessica promised, "I'll try and find it."

"Another thing. Have you at any time, for any reason, tried to get in touch with her?"

"No, I considered her a bitch, and I believe in letting sleeping dogs lie." Her eyes rolled toward the stove. "The coffee's made. You men drink it—I got to lie down and rest now."

"You drink it," I said to Swede.

I left by the front door and hiked up Superior to Terminal. The white T-bird had flown. I drove downtown and parked behind the *Globe*. No white T-bird had alighted there. Entering by the pressroom door, I saw that Lem Bergstrom was linotyping. I descended to the basement lab and delivered the Graphic filmholder to Leo.

He remembered, I didn't.

"Hey, show you the joke on Harvey Staples."

He showed me the photograph of Game Warden Bowers pointing out the hole in the ice to Willie Popke and Doc Soole. In the background and off to one corner, the flash had reached a fourth figure.

The pix revealed a slightly out-of-focus Harvey Staples in the act of slipping a slightly out-of-focus fish into the top of his hip boot. The fish was a wall-eyed pike Harvey had managed to flip up onto the ice and kick out of sight among the packing boxes.

"The paper didn't run this," I said.

"No, I routed it out of the engraving. But taking a game fish out of season could've cost Harvey fifty dollars and sixty days. I've been saving the print to see the look on his face."

"Let me have that pleasure, Leo."

Upstairs, I reduced the day's intake to an obit notice and a news story. I worded the obituary so that Ralph Riker was survived by Jessica and by an earlier wife, Mrs. Babe Riker of St. Louis, Missouri. The news story said that due to failing eyesight, Olin Wolff was retiring from his position as treasurer of the Co-op.

Both pieces of reportage I laid on Ed Horace's desk. He read the obit first and raised fever-reddened eyes. "You must mean Bebe—there's no such name as Babe. And former, not earlier."

"She may not be former, but the legal wife."

Ed whistled.

Then he read the Olin Wolff story, twice. "How come Olin announced his retirement just at this particular time?"

"He just handed it out along with a cigar," I said. "What's the next assignment, boss?"

"It came over the news-ticker the post-mortem

on Ralph Riker indicated death from carbon dioxide poisoning."

"Don't you mean carbon monoxide?"

"It said carbon dioxide. You might check on that with Walter Burch."

I decided to check it with Doc Soole instead. He had an office across the street from the public library, with a half-dozen patients conning the waiting room copies of *Life* and *The Readers' Digest*. They glared as the girl let me go in out of turn.

Doc Soole left another patient in his examining room to join me in a cubicle, where he stood surrounded by drying X-ray films.

"Cases of carbon dioxide poisoning occur every so often," said the coroner. "I remember being called to treat a Hay Center farmer all of twelve, fifteen years ago. He got dizzy and keeled over in the silo. Carbon dioxide is manufactured by the process of breathing, by the decay of vegetation, and by fermentation. It's heavier by half than air and settles to the bottom of wells and silos. A strong concentration causes spasms of the glottis, convulsions, and death from respiratory paralysis."

"How do you tell it from carbon monoxide poisoning?"

"Monoxide is the easy one. It combines with the hemoglobin, creating carboxyhemoglobin, resulting in the characteristic cherry color of the blood. The cherry color remains even to the point of body putrefaction. In carbon dioxide deaths the blood is dark red; there isn't much to go on aside from the evidences of asphyxiation. I'm just as glad Riker wasn't dumped on my doorstep."

"Maybe he was and you hauled him to Larksdale to avoid doing the autopsy?"

"I might have pulled him through. I saved the Hay Center case."

"How long had he been in the silo?"

"It happened ten, twelve years ago," Doc Soole repeated. "It's my recollection he was doing the evening chores. He didn't answer the dinner bell. He might have been unconscious ten or twenty minutes before the hired man found him, and another half-hour before I reached the scene."

"And he was still alive, still breathing." I watched Soole's thin face and picked my words with care— the five-thousand reward hung in the balance. "Suppose a person was overpowered, tied hand and foot, and dumped in the locked trunk of a car. Could he manage to manufacture enough carbon dioxide to kill himself?"

"I imagine he'd be more likely to suffocate from lack of oxygen, Ken."

"At any rate, he could pass out? And next assume he was taken into a small room containing a gas stove, and the stove was turned on but not lighted? Couldn't he inhale enough carbon monoxide to induce carboxyhemoglobin and cherry-colored blood?"

He studied me out of keen eyes. "Where is the stove?"

"There are stoves all over town." I might have

added there was one in the "Valhalla" cottage, too.

"Bottled-gas stoves, and the gas is either butane or propane. Propane is the cold weather fuel because it vaporizes at lower temperatures. Propane and butane are harmless. The stuff that kills people is city gas, natural gas, pipeline gas. It contains carbon monoxide."

Sheriff Popke sat at the roll-top desk in the jail office. On the desk was a baseball autographed by Roy Campanella, kept covered by an upside-down goldfish bowl since Campanella's injury. Popke had been on the phone with Lieutenant Hendryx.

"Jessie Riker could have tied herself up, and they figured she might have, but she wasn't faking the effects of shock and exposure. Then they found the car keys and a pair of woman's kid gloves thrown away behind the filling station. The gloves were too small for Jessie. There was adhesive-tape stickum all over them and old stains that proved to be human blood. There were traces of old bloodstains in the car, but no fingerprints."

The sheriff studied the Campanella souvenir as if it were a crystal ball. "I got an anonymous phone call from Wydota to the effect Harvey Staples killed Ralph Riker. It turned out Harvey spent the whole evening in a Wydota poolhall, boiled as an owl. I'm glad I didn't have to bring him in—he stinks up the jail."

FIFTEEN

In Wydota, the shadows were lengthening, the promise of spring balm in the air yielding to the pinch of the aproaching winter evening. The thermometer outside the Mud Hen station read thirty degrees, again below freezing. I stepped inside and gazed through the ticket grating at the agent on duty. He returned the gaze with a glance from under the green shade that sheltered his neat, pale, complete-stranger's face.

"Where's Les?" I said.

"Mr. Jopperman is taking a week's vacation. I'm the replacement. Something I can do for you?"

"Les was here last night—"

"Oh, he's here nights. He's merely taking the days off to get in some winter fishing."

I drove rapidly to Oak Lake over the county gravel, the township dirt, and the short-cut through Ralph Riker's rented cornfield. From the top of the slope I saw the distant dots of the Busch Brothers truck and packing boxes. They were now seining the far end of the lake.

Much closer were a solitary fish shanty, a broken-fendered jalopy, and Les Jopperman's coupe.

I steered down the slope, past the violated muskrat

lodes, out onto the ice. At that point I shut off the motor and started hiking.

The ice sheet ahead was pitted with holes, roughly a yard apart, creating the effect of a giant's Chinese-checker game. The holes close to the shanty were agleam with unfrozen water. They had been chopped today.

The fish shanty stood jerry-built of unpainted sheathing, mounted on fence-post skids, and attached by a log chain to the rear bumper of Les Jopperman's car. I opened the strap-hinged door.

"Any luck?"

In the kerosene-lantern-lighted interior, two faces peered at me. One was Les's kewpie countenance, ringed in raccoon fur. The other belonged to Harvey Staples, who crouched beside a hole in the shanty's ice floor. His mittened hands grasped what appeared to be the handle of a fish-spear stuck in the water.

"You fellows are doing this all wrong," I said. "Chop a hole, muddy up the water, move on to the next hole. What kind of fishing is that?"

Harvey Staples straightened dangerously. He was a rawhide-tough six-footer who seemed to have last washed his face when he shaved it. He had last shaved before going to jail. As he stepped toward me, he brought with him an aura of dead fish, of trapped wild animals, of the gook used to bait traps, and of Harvey Staples himself.

"Go to hell," he said. "Mind your own damn business. Beat it."

He was not a man of subtle speech or high intelligence. Hardly bright enough to tell carbon dioxide from carbon monoxide.

"Or what?" I said. "You'll sneak up behind me some dark night and clobber me when I'm not looking?"

The unwhiskered part of Harvey's face turned a kind of pool-table green.

"Huh?" he said.

I could have enlightened him by explaining that I knew my camera had caught him bootlegging the wall-eye, that he'd slugged me and stolen the wrong filmholder. What changed my mind was a glimpse of the kaleidoscopic reactions sliding over Les Jopperman's face. He looked startled, uncertain, and finally pleased.

I decided Les could not be happy in the same fish shanty with Harvey.

"Les saw you," I said. "I can send you up for assault and battery, maybe even attempted murder. You left me unconscious to die in the thirty-below cold."

The accusation wounded Harvey. He began, "I knocked on the door—"

"Yes, you gave me that much of a break, and maybe I'll give you a break. Go sit in your car while I talk things over with Les."

Harvey Staples shrugged and walked out of the shanty. It struck me he gave up easily.

Leslie, I expected, wouldn't be so easy.

I began by lifting the spear out of the water. Only it wasn't a spear. The shaft extended well out through the shanty door by the time I got the business end out of the hole. The business end was a hay hook. A hay hook is used in handling baled hay. This one, lashed to the shaft, resembled a foot-long fishhook made of finger-thick iron.

I contemplated it. "Trying to catch a whale, a Loch Ness monster?" I asked.

Les's chapped face formed a pained, resigned smile. "I won't beat around the bush with you, Kenny. You know as well as I do, Gladys Irvine's suitcases were never found. I assumed the murderer probably dumped them into the lake along with her body."

"So you blistered your hands and took in Staples as your podner to do the heavy work?"

"He muscled in. I imagine he has hopes of finding the missing Co-op money."

"You didn't want him around? Is that why you told me he could have killed Riker?"

"Well, Kenny, he could have. He was out here with me yesterday. He left here early, around four o'clock. He could have been in Milquevais in time to kill Ralph."

I fancied Les had done his best to sic Harvey onto Ralph. I could imagine him explaining to Harvey Staples how the muskrat-trapper had been double-crossed.

"What did *you* hope to find in Gladys' suitcases?" I said.

"Oh, a clue."

"Such as?"

"Her sister's name and address, for one thing."

"Gladys had no sister."

"Whoever the woman was," said Les. "I'm just throwing out ideas."

"You're good at it. Now let me try. Do you remember interviewing Jessica Riker and what she told you about Gladys making those summer week-end trips to Minneapolis?"

Leslie nodded.

"Did you check the story at the station in Milquevais?" I asked.

"Oh, sure. There's no doubt that Jessica did take Gladys to the station, that Gladys bought a ticket, that she got on the train, and also that she returned on the Sunday night train."

"A round trip to Minneapolis, or just a one-way ticket?"

Leslie hesitated. "I didn't think of asking," he said.

Up to that point, I'd had nothing to go on—except the twelve-hundred-dollar withdrawal and Ralph Riker's habit of violating the Sabbath.

I said, "Go back to the start. You felt sure *Bloody Murder Magazine* wouldn't go for a case where a hick sheriff got a lucky tip and made the arrest right off the bat. You wanted to inject mystery and menace, build up a bogeyman blowing poison gas into sleeping beauties' bedrooms. You figured you could horse around with it, and then straighten everything out with an anonymous tip."

Leslie licked his lips and didn't like the taste.

"The tip was this," I said. "Gladys never changed

trains at Indian Rock. Her week ends were spent here at Oak Lake. On Sunday nights she bought her ticket and boarded the train at Wydota."

Leslie's mouth moved. No word came out.

"A little louder," I said.

The mouth moved again. The words came out: "If I knew so much, why haven't I claimed the reward before now?"

"The reward changed things. Your information became worth five thousand bucks. Only you couldn't come forward with what you had known all along. People would know you must have known it all along. The railroad would can you, just as they'd can you for coining a profit out of the information in the telegrams you handle. Walter Burch might can you for withholding evidence. He may yet."

Les did not give up easily. "I may have sold some woman the tickets," he said. "I did not recognize the body as being hers. Nobody recognized Gladys for days."

"It wasn't just Gladys."

He waited for the worst.

"Gladys didn't hike the five miles from the lake," I said. "Somebody brought her to the station, and you knew the guy."

Leslie started as if a mousetrap had snapped under his nose. "Guy? It was a woman—a woman driving some kind of little foreign car."

The mousetrap snapped under *my* nose. I'd been so damned sure it'd been Ralph Riker who'd spent the week ends with Gladys.

"What woman? Who was she?"

"Just some dame who drove up at night, unloaded a passenger, and drove away. Honestly, Kenny, the main thing I hope to find in the suitcases is a clue to her identity—"

I walked over to the broken-fendered jalopy and the aromatic Harvey Staples.

"Smart cookie, that Jopperman," said Harvey. He must have observed how I felt.

"Ralph Riker was a smart cookie, too," I said. "You wouldn't turn to Les for practical advice, would you? Now, Ralph impressed me as being a guy who'd been around, shipped to sea, rammed about the country. *His* advice would be worth listening to."

"That's for sure."

"Look, Harvey, I want to ask you this. Did you tell Ralph at the time how you heard the car out here on the lake before Christmas?"

"Yeah, I told him. I said I might have to lay off the trapping—it looked like the warden was laying for me."

"What'd he think of it?"

"He figured it wasn't the warden—more likely somebody stealing the rats from my traps. His idea was I should pull up my traps, let the other guy set his, and steal *his* rats."

"That's the kind of a smart cookie I took Ralph to be." He had stubbed his toe over some commandment other than the sixth and the ninth, was all. I had no idea which. I felt like giving up.

"You're going to have to give the filmholder back, Harvey," I said.

Harvey looked confused.

"The thingamajig you swiped out of my camera."

"I ain't got it here," said Harvey, "It's in the sh-garage at home."

"I'll follow you home."

At least, I wouldn't have to smell him all the way into town.

Following Harvey's jalopy through the cornfield and along the roads, I brooded about Ralph Riker having known since before Christmas of the mysterious car on the Oak Lake ice. He had never breathed a word about it. Harvey Staples couldn't have told, not without exposing his illicit trapping. That didn't hold true for Ralph. Ralph had squealed on Harvey *before* Gladys' body was found. So what had kept him from mentioning the mystery car?

I was still struggling with these things like an amateur juggler trying to keep six pie plates in the air when we entered Wydota.

Harvey turned his jalopy into a side street, one that in summer would have been pleasant with the shade of trees.

Harvey braked in front of a house, waved a hand at me, and sprinted up a shoveled walk beside the house.

I parked behind the jalopy and looked at the house. It was white-painted, with a bay window. The sash was green, the curtains yellow. A child's face parted the curtains. The child's nose flattened into a blob against the glass. A hand snatched the kid away. A piece of cloth appeared and carefully polished away the smudge left by the young nose. A couple of twitches restored the yellow curtains to prim, starched straightness.

If Mrs. Staples kept house like this, I could not imagine her even letting Mr. Staples inside the door.

I jumped out of the Chevie and also ran up the shoveled path. It led me past the house to a garage at the rear of the lot. Behind the garage ran an alley, and across the alley was a backyard furnished with a tool shed, a chicken coop, three rain barrels, a baby carriage half-buried in a snowdrift, and the back view of a dwelling leaking rust stains from the nails in the siding.

Aside from the snow, the layout resembled a less desirable residence in Tijuana.

I rushed across the alley to the tool shed. Its half-opened door showed a rocking chair with one rocker missing, an alarm clock spilling its steel-spring entrails, a lawnmower. There were other things, including a workbench on which lay a pile of shingles shaped for stretching muskrat hides, a skinning knife, and some rusted Victor traps.

Harvey Staples knelt beneath the workbench fumbling with something. I stepped inside the shed to see what. Harvey's fingers were sorting through the contents of a suitcase—bras, panties, nylons, frozen wads and wisps like family wash that had blown off the clothesline into the mud. He found the filmholder, and after that found a whisky bottle, which he uncapped and tilted up to drain of a possible last drop.

Head tilted up to the bottle, he saw me watching.

This time Harvey didn't give up so easily.

He caught at the workbench, pulled himself erect —and his hand snaked across the bench and grabbed the skinning knife.

He came at me.

He came faster than I could back away, and the junk in the shed left no space for side-stepping. I snatched the alarm clock and slammed its steel-spring guts into Harvey's face.

He kept coming on, but blindly, and tripped over the lawnmower. Trying to save his balance, he dropped the knife.

"You're going to get hurt, Harvey," I said.

He stopped to think things over.

"Did you find only the one suitcase?" I said. "Does Les Jopperman know about it?"

Harvey must have decided I was all talk, a man of words instead of actions. He bent over, reaching for the knife.

I hit him a dirty rabbit punch at the base of the skull.

SIXTEEN

We all develop habit patterns, such as frequenting pool halls or bowling alleys, brooding behind locked doors, playing with pipestems, entering box-top contests, playing solitaire, raising rose gardens, living in squalor, saving money. Perhaps even writing books and painting pictures are essentially matters of habit.

I called Ed Horace from a Wydota filling station—I was forming the habit of using filling-station phones.

"I've found a suitcase," I said.

Ed croaked like a bull frog.

"It's a woman's suitcase of the airline fabric type, originally light tan in color, now very water-stained. Water-soaked, really, and so's everything in it. The contents include size-9 hosiery, size-5 panties, 36B bras, a dress labeled Neusteter's and another labeled Dayton's, and—"

"There's a Neusteter's in Denver," said Ed.

"How do you know?"

"I worked on a paper there."

Working on papers can get to be a habit, too.

"—empty whisky bottle," I said, "toothbrush, hairbrush, comb, three paperback novels with the pages stuck together, a traveler's electric iron, two bricks, and a film of Oak Lake mud over everything."

"Where would Gladys have got a dress with a Denver store label?"

"I know a fellow who buys his clothes at church white-elephant bazaars," I said. "By the way, any calls or callers for me?"

"Three women phoned. Your wife wants to know will you be home for dinner. Florrie Schultz said to remind you tonight's the Thursday Pen Club. The other didn't give her name—just said the snapshot was found."

"Call Kelly back and tell her I can't make it for dinner. The reason is, you've given me an assignment in Minneapolis."

Ed started raving, a habit of managing editors. He wanted to know what the hell and why the hell—

"I'm filling the gas tank and charging it on the *Globe* credit card," I said. "You can't fire me. If you do, the Old Man will deduct his fifteen-a-week from your salary."

The two-hour trek ended after dark in front of a brick-faced apartment near the Walker Gallery. The tight foyer had one wall of built-in mailboxes and a punch-button call-board of tenant names.

Shelton-Grimstead occupied 326.

I poked buttons at random, received an answering buzz, and pushed open the foyer's inner door. I lugged the water-damaged suitcase up the flights of carpeted stairs and rapped on 326. The door opened enough to disclose a glimpse of a healthy-looking, competent-looking, secretarial-looking young woman."

"Miss Grimstead?" I guessed.

"We never buy from peddlers."

"Miss Grimstead, I'd like to see Miss Shelton—"

"And agents aren't allowed in the building."

"—about Dirk Lebijohn."

Eva must have overheard. Her face replaced Miss Grimstead's in the crack of doorway. For the first time I noticed the color of Eva's hair. It was bronze.

"Oh, it's you. I don't think I care to discuss Dirk with a report—"

"Then do you recognize this?" I held up the suit-case.

"No, I don't. What's the gag?"

"It contains things you may be able to identify as the property of Gladys Irvine."

"Oh. Well, you can step inside." Eva opened the door. At once I ceased noticing the color of her hair. Who cares about an Aphrodite of Cyrene's complexion and coiffure? This goddess frowned at the suit-case.

"Don't put that filthy thing down. I'll get a news-paper to spread."

I took a novelist's interest in watching her cross the apartment. An accurate description of Eva's walk would have sold a million copies of a book. She vanished into the kitchenette before I thought of the right words, though.

"You can dream, buster," said Miss Grimstead, sneering.

Maybe the sneer was to cover up an inferiority com-plex.

Eva Shelton returned with a yesterday's Minneapolis Journal and a folded slip of memo paper. The folded slip she pushed at Miss Grimstead. "Here's the list of things to get from the corner delicatessen."

Miss Grimstead looked surprised.

"You better hurry, Debby, before they close."

Miss Grimstead shot a look at the memo and hurried out the door.

It was all right with me; I felt glad to see her go.

Eva Shelton spread the newspaper over the top of a coffee table. I placed the suitcase on the newspaper and opened it up.

Eva Shelton rapidly and expertly inventoried the contents.

"Gladys didn't drink, and she could never have worn these things."

"She'd reduced."

"Reducing doesn't shrink feet. She couldn't have gotten her feet in number-9 hosiery. Besides, these are extra-longs—tall girl's."

"You're a tall girl."

Eva pecked thumb and forefinger into the bristles of the brush. She had slim hands with tapering fingers. She found a hair in the brush.

"I'm not a peroxide blonde."

"Well, to tell the truth, I really didn't think this was your stuff or Gladys' either. I mostly wanted to talk to you when Dirk Lebijohn wasn't around."

"About what?"

"About Dirk Lebijohn."

Eva frowned. "I'm rather fond of Dirk. He's different. You mustn't judge him by ordinary standards."

"He may look different to you," I said, "by my standards he's just another Harvey Staples."

"The name sounds familiar. Oh, I remember. The trapper."

"Harvey's a trapper because he's psychologically unadjusted to holding down a steady job. He can't be bothered with neckties and shoeshines. He's hot-tempered; he gets into fights. He hopes to get rich by finding money at the bottom of a lake or at the foot of a rainbow. Harvey's a very common type of small-town bum."

Indignation welled in Eva Shelton's eyes. "Dirk's an artist," she said.

"He's an artist because that justifies him in being a law unto himself. It enables him to feel morally superior to everyone else. He's a big-city, Left Bank, *avant garde* bum."

"All the same, if I'm remembered a hundred years from now, it'll be because Dirk Lebijohn painted me."

I seemed to see a mirror with Kelly and Florrie Schultz in it. "You're saying that because you feel there's got to be something more to life than doing dishes and making beds, taking dictation and pounding a typewriter. Along comes a beatnik with a Van Gogh gleam in his eye, and he promises to land you in the Louvre a hundred years from now. Be careful he doesn't land you behind bars, Eva."

"For what?"

"For renting that cottage at Oak Lake. For hauling Gladys to board the train at Wydota."

She lulled before the storm. Then she stormed: "I don't have to explain myself to you!"

"You'd rather explain yourself to the Milquevais sheriff and county attorney?"

"You think you can make a lot of trouble for me, don't you?"

I said, "People make trouble for themselves. All I do is write up the pertinent facts for the newspaper. The question is whether your actions were pertinent to the murder of Gladys Irvine."

She was shaking her head when the telephone pealed out in the kitchenette.

She went to answer it, walking in her indescribable manner. I heard her say "Hello," and later "I'll do my best," and after that "Probably half an hour."

She came back.

"That was the model agency," she explained. "They're rounding up candidates for a Miss Icicle contest. I told them I was busy and I'd call them back in half an hour." She sat down on a divan beyond the coffee table and suitcase. She said, "The answer to your question is, Gladys was more or less crazy. She got that way from brooding over all those old papers of her mother's. What set her off was the fact the papers gave her absolutely no kind of a line on her old man. He seemed to have just popped up out of nowhere back in '30.

"Of course, that was during the Depression, the hard times. The country swarmed with homeless, jobless men. Charles Irvine could have deserted a wife and family somewhere. He could have been an ex-con. He could have escaped from a lunatic asylum. But Gladys, being Gladys, had to make him a figure of romantic mystery."

I sensed what was coming, but the mistake about Ralph Riker had made me leary of throwing out guesses. I waited.

"Gladys," said Eva Shelton, "decided that Charles Irvine and Charles Holadare must be one and the same man."

"On what evidence?"

"The same first names. The fact Holadare disappeared the year before Irvine popped up. The coincidence they were both radio technicians."

I asked questions: "Photographs? Fingerprints?"

Eva Shelton gave answers: "The only picture of Irvine was a police photo of him with his face half shot away. Charles Holadare's fingerprints aren't on record."

"Signatures? Samples of handwriting?"

"Gladys had practically nothing, and the little she had she took to Helen Holadare. You see, Gladys was a daydreaming, impractical person. She was surprised and shocked when Helen Holadare threw the stuff in the fireplace and threatened to have Gladys arrested for fraud and imposture."

I mused, "In effect, Gladys was claiming to be Holadare's daughter by his second, legal marriage, and therefore an heir—"

"Gladys wasn't the kind to fight for her rights, though."

"What kind was she?"

"The sulk-in-the-corner kind."

"She didn't go to a lawyer?"

"She went back to Milquevais. I think probably she was afraid of testing her case in court, afraid of seeing her dream reduced to ashes. At least, that's the impression I got from Midge."

"How'd Midge get into it?"

Eva Shelton shrugged. "Midge wasn't married then, only engaged, with Helen Holadare doing her utmost to break off the engagement. I think she intended to fight the old lady with every weapon in the book."

"I mean, how did Midge find out about Gladys?"

"Probably Mother Holadare said something to Jim that he repeated to Midge."

"Go on."

"Well, Midge knew me. She knew of Dirk's interest in hypnotism. She thought a hypnotized Gladys might remember some buried childhood clues about Charles Irvine." A pause. "Gladys was willing. And Dirk needed the money."

"What was in it for *you?*"

Eva seemed surprised. "Nothing. They were all my friends—Midge, Dirk, and Gladys. Maybe I'm a born baby-sitter by instinct." She thought awhile. "Another thing, I wanted to see Jim Holadare escape from under his mother's thumb.

"I drove up Friday evenings with Dirk," she went on. "We picked up Gladys at Indian Rock. Gladys and I shared the cottage bedroom. Dirk slept on the daybed. He usually hypnotized Gladys once on Saturday and again on Sunday. Then, Sunday night, I took her to Wydota—she had a terror of being late and missing the train on account of a flat tire. If we missed it at Wydota, it wouldn't be so far to drive her to Milquevais."

Eva gave the impression of loosening up and volunteering details.

"How'd you come to pick 'Valhalla'?"

"We had to meet somewheres. We couldn't operate under the Rikers' noses. The cottage was close by, and it was cheap. Midge wasn't rolling in money, and to raise cash she hocked her ring."

"Pawnbrokers report their pledges to the police," I pointed out. "The police check those reports against lists of lost and stolen articles. She *gave* Dirk the ring, didn't she?"

"She may have given it to him to keep until she could raise the money," Eva Shelton said.

"Any idea where he kept it?"

"Not the faintest. He never had a bank box in his life. He might have stuck it away in a coffee can, under the mattress, somewhere he wouldn't lose it."

"Could he have stuck it away behind the washstand in the cottage?"

Eva Shelton considered the suggestion. "It could be," she said. "Dirk isn't too regular about paying his rent. He's been locked out of his studio any number

of times. He's had quite a bit of experience with land-
lords taking his clothes and paints and everything.
So if he had the ring, he might have felt the cottage
was as safe a place as any."

"All right. What happened?"

"It just didn't work out. Gladys did her best, and
she would have climbed Mount Everest on her hands
and knees. Only she didn't remember any more hypnotized than wide awake. And then Jim and Midge
were married, so Midge lost interest in financing
the experiment."

"Perhaps she also lost interest in paying Lebijohn
any money? Kept putting him off, letting him keep
the ring?"

"I don't see why you keep harping on the ring,"
Eva Shelton said. "The point is, all this happened
last summer. Gladys wasn't killed until New Year's,
so there's no connection."

I closed the suitcase and wrapped my fingers around
the handle. "If that's so, I'll be running along." I expected Eva to stall. The half-hour wasn't nearly ended.

She stood up, and with her fluid-asset walk moved
ahead of me to the door. I thought she would think
of something with her hand on the knob. She fooled
me by opening the door.

"Let me know if you ever find out who the suitcase
belonged to," she said.

"I'll send you an autographed copy of my story in
the *Globe*."

I carried the suitcase down the hall, down the flights
of stairs, through the foyer into the street.

I looked up and down the street.

There was no corner delicatessen, no white T-bird parked along the curb, nobody in sight except a man walking a large dog across the street.

I had been so damned sure Eva had sent the Grimstead girl to phone Dirk Lebijohn. Just as sure as I'd been that Ralph Riker met the trains at Wydota.

I stepped from the curb, shifted the suitcase to my left hand, and reached the right hand to the Chevie's door handle.

Just as I did so, the dog leaped from out of nowhere to close his jaws on my right wrist. He didn't bite the wrist, just held onto it.

I looked into his gleaming, moon-satellite eyes.

"Down, Count!" I said.

The canine jaws tightened slightly.

James Holadare came ranging across the pavement. "It's the Count's way of asking for a lift," he said.

So much more genteel and refined than a gun in the ribs—so much quieter than a gun, too.

"Hop in," I said, giving up easily.

SEVENTEEN

Holadare gave the directions. I followed them carefully, because of the Weimaraner standing on the seat behind and breathing on the back of my neck. A traffic collision, even a sudden braking to avoid a collision, might have made him grab the neck in his teeth. For the same reason I spoke in a respectfully polite voice:

"Miss Shelton seems to be a very loyal employee."

He mused before answering. "The Holadare Company tries to merit the loyalty of its employees."

"I suppose you pay top salaries with paid vacations and medical and hospital benefits, plus pensions. Plus rewards in the case of murdered ex-employees."

I braked for a changing light I would normally have run through.

"Gladys Irvine earned $350 a month with us, Svederup. I imagine she received a similar salary from the Co-op. I'm sure over the past half-dozen years her living expenses amounted to less than half her earnings. You figure it out."

I counted on my fingers until the light changed. Estimating other people's assets was becoming a habit.

"She may have socked away seven or eight thousand," I suggested.

"In round figures. My own computations are somewhat more exact. I believe Gladys had a nest egg of $7420."

"No odd cents?"

"And I'll tell you how I worked it out," James Holadare said. "Seven thousand four hundred and twenty dollars plus the $2580 taken from the Co-op would equal $10,000."

"Did you peek in the back of the book to find that solution?"

"Yes, a psychology book. Con men and shake-down artists—and I stress the word artists—seem to deal in large round sums. Turn right at the next block."

I turned, gently.

"In multiples of fifty-dollar bills?" I turned my head and felt the Weimaraner's breath fan my ear. James Holadare beside me looked nearly as tall as a seated Lincoln statue; he wore a statue's carved-in-stone expression, too. I couldn't tell whether he knew Midge had paid off in fifty-dollar bills.

"You talked to Miss Shelton," he said. "Isn't it evident to you that around Thanksgiving Dirk Lebijohn again made contact with Gladys, and this time she paid the freight and he took her for a cool ten thousand?"

We crossed several streets. The pavement climbed slightly, leveled off, and dropped away toward the frozen spread of Lake Harriet.

"You're a systems-analysis expert, and you're exact when it comes to mathematics. I'm a newspaperman. I'm exact when it comes to words." I made a left turn without being told. "Nothing is evident to me without evidence. Lacking evidence, your allegations add up to criminal libel and slander of Dirk Lebijohn."

We came abreast of the Robber Baron castle.

"Stop," said James Holadare, "and I'll show you the evidence."

"It won't be necessary for the dog to lead me by the wrist," I said.

Holadare had a key to the fortress door. He guided me through the front hallway and switched up the lights in the first large room we entered. Gesturing, he asked, "Notice anything about the pictures here?"

I failed the test.

"They've been cleaned," Holadare said. "Midge employed Lebijohn to clean the picture that hangs over her mantel. Mother was impressed. She employed the fellow to do the same here." He steered me across the room and stopped. "I call your attention to this one."

This one looked vaguely familiar.

"My mother as a young woman," Holadare said. "Lebijohn cleaned this portrait over the Thanksgiving week end. He took it with him over the week end. Come on, Count."

He, the dog, and I entered the next room.

"Notice anything?" said Holadare.

I passed the test. "Uncleaned."

"Yes, because Lebijohn could no longer be bothered with such menial tasks. He had come into money —Gladys Irvine's money." Holadare made the point like seven no trump in bridge.

"I'm afraid a judge wouldn't consider it admissible evidence," I said.

"Wait until you've heard my mother's story."

He escorted me into a library. It had bookshelves instead of pictures around the walls. Otherwise, it was like the rest of the place, a museum lacking only the velvet ropes. Even the fire in the open hearth looked artificial and hostile. Maybe it was chilled by Helen Holadare's presence.

Mrs. Holadare sat in a thronelike chair, browsing through a book—possibly a volume on wedded bliss by that old marriage counselor, Aristotle.

"Mother, this is Mr. Svederup of the Milquevais *Globe*," said James Holadare.

"I've met Mr. Svederup."

Holadare brushed his cowlick from surprised eyes. Apparently his mother had not told him all.

"I've decided to make a statement to the press," Helen Holadare was saying.

I asked, "May I have the Count's permission to take pencil and paper from my pocket?"

"Go ahead," she said.

"And sit down to take my notes?"

She nodded. I sat down at a museum-piece table.

Helen Holadare began talking. "A man named Lebijohn came to my home last night. He is an indigent pseudo-artist and a self-taught practitioner of hypnotism. He claimed that under his hypnotic spell

Gladys Irvine, shortly before her death, succeeded in recalling in detail her father's death during a supposed holdup. He further claimed that Gladys had been able to identify the killer."

"A little slower." I wanted to get this down word for word.

Mrs. Holadare went on: "For this information, Lebijohn demanded the sum of five thousand dollars. He professed to feel it solved the Gladys Irvine case. He inferred that Gladys was killed to prevent her from denouncing the murderer."

"Did he name the guilty person?"

"He did not, and if he had, the Count would have torn him to pieces. However, a couple of hours ago I received a long-distance call from a man purporting to be Lebijohn. He said there had been no radio-shop holdup in 1934. Charles Irvine was killed by a woman. Gladys Irvine made the identification of the killer from a painting of me as a young woman."

She said it all in an utterly flat, unemotional voice. She might have been a teacher keeping me in after school, dictating an exercise I had to copy fifty times on the blackboard.

"You understand this isn't evidence against mother," burst from James Holadare. "Gladys may never have said these things. If she did say them, she did so under the influence of Lebijohn's hypnotic suggestion. No court would accept such testimony, except as proof of Lebijohn's intention to extort money."

"Be quiet, James, I'm speaking." Helen Holadare used the tone she would have used to the dog. Her son subsided exactly as the dog would have subsided.

She went on: "Lebijohn asserted that I killed Charles Irvine because he was in reality my former husband, Charles Holadare. I wanted him out of the way so I could have him declared legally dead in order to probate the will and obtain control of the Holadare Company."

"Uh-huh."

"At the next step, Lebijohn claimed, he communicated these so-called facts to my daughter-in-law, who communicated them to my son, who in turn communicated them to me." For the first time the flat voice was flawed by a note of uncertainty.

I raised my eyes to hers. Hers were old and tired, in the cobweb pattern of the time tracks that had suddenly appeared on her face.

"I'm supposed to have conspired with my son," she said. "James is supposed to have gone to Milquevais on New Year's Eve and to have killed and buried Gladys Irvine."

I glanced at James Holadare. He looked like an old oil painting badly in need of cleaning.

"New Year's Eve is traditionally a quiet family occasion with us," he said. "I spent it here in this house, with my mother."

"And your wife?"

"Midge refused to come. She doesn't get along with mother."

He had no alibi.

Helen Holadare said, "Lebijohn also contends that James went to Milquevais yesterday, kidnaped Mrs.

Riker and murdered Riker, and concealed Riker's body in a closet off the entrance hallway to his home, to be dragged out in the presence of party guests with the assertion that the body had been found on the front step." Again my glance strayed to James Holadare. He had got out a handkerchief and was toweling his face.

"I drove up to Milquevais yesterday afternoon," he said. "I went to the banks and dropped in to see Olin and Swedenborg Wolff."

"About what?"

"I was trying to find out whether Gladys had money in any of the banks, whether she had been buying government savings bonds through an employee purchase plan. As I told you, I'm convinced Gladys had savings of $7420, but I could find no trace of a bank account or bonds—"

"How long were you in Milquevais?"

"I would say from three in the afternoon to five o'clock." He swallowed. "I swear I had nothing to do with Riker's death."

He had no alibi, though.

I looked at the old lady. "Lebijohn told you all this on the phone. How did you reply?" I asked.

"I defied him to take his wild and unfounded accusations to the county attorney in Milquevais. At the time, I did not know of my son's trip yesterday. I assumed Lebijohn was simply trying to blackmail me with insane, empty threats."

"You say *at the time*. You've changed your mind since?"

"I have. I now realize these allegations might lead to my son's being charged with murder. Even if found not guilty, he might live the rest of his life under a cloud of suspicion. It's my duty as a mother to forestall such a tragedy by nipping it in the bud."

Her voice had risen. It brought the dog to his feet, stiff-legged, a rumbling in his throat.

"Mr. Svederup, believe me. From the day James was born, my actions have been governed by the dictates of his best interests. I've endeavored to create and conserve an estate, to achieve a social position, to see him happily married to a suitable wife. I sought to spare him what I've been through. I know from experience what it is to be penniless, to be eyed askance by one's neighbors, to be married to an improvident and profligate man who consorted with thugs and wasted the family substance at the gambling table."

Helen Holadare arose from her chair—we were all on our feet.

"I couldn't possibly have killed Charles Irvine in 1934 under the impression he was Charles Holadare," she said. "I couldn't because five years before, in 1929, I had already killed my husband. I killed him because he was a drunken, dissolute crook engaged in gambling away the assets of the Holadare Company. I killed him to stop him from blighting and ruining my son's future."

EIGHTEEN

The roadside sign proclaimed, ENTERING MILQUE-
VAIS— Ahead loomed the glass-block and plate-glass
Farmers Cooperative Creamery, made small by
Northern lights flickering in the winter night's sky. It
looked like a Hollywood premiere, or a torchlight
parade to welcome home the country cousin.

I wondered what I had done to deserve my luck,
why Helen Holadare had given *me* the story of her
thirty-years-past crime before giving herself up to the
cops.

She wanted good front-page coverage in the Cheese
Capital of the World, I thought. Gladys Irvine and
Ralph Riker had met their deaths in Milquevais
County, and the suspected slayer would go on trail in
the local courthouse before a jury of *Globe* readers.
Maybe she suspected that James Holadare would be
the guy on trial?

Say that Gladys' "memory" was sheer fantasy,
the wish-fullfilment dream of a brooding mind, a fic-
tion conceived in resentment of Helen Holadare
and born in the twilight sleep of hypnosis.

I could see Dirk Lebijohn taking the fantasy at face
value—believing it, the way I believed Ralph Riker
met the trains at Wydota.

Murder's a mirror, one in which everyone looks like everyone else.

I fancied Lebijohn needing money, the way I'd needed it in Tijuana. I pictured him going to Midge Holadare, the way I'd gone to Old Man Crossway. It wasn't blackmail; it was merely selling information he had and she wanted to buy.

The mirror flashed; it showed me Midge and James Holadare quarreling. They looked like Kelly and Ken Svederup quarreling. I remembered Kelly bawling me out for paying too much attention to Eva Shelton. Midge might have bawled her husband out about paying too much attention to his mother: *I won't welcome in my New Year with that woman. I know what she is—*

And James Holadare could have traveled to Milquevais and silenced Gladys—done it to protect his mother without consulting her.

Now the aurora borealis vanished, blotted out by the Co-op's bulk. I slowed, stared up at the slits of light streaking the Venetian-blinded windows of the treasurer's office.

Another mirror! I saw old Olin Wolff looking like the reflection of Helen Holadare. Olin, too, had been trying to provide for a son's future.

Swede's future looked to me as dubious as James Holadare's. There might be a courtroom and a jury ahead of him, too. It depended on how much he'd known and overlooked or covered up, trying to keep the secret of his old man's dimming eyesight.

Beyond the Co-op, Terminal Avenue stretched

away, dipped through the Mud Hen underpass, and met with Superior Street.

Here, the lighted window was a kitchen one. I parked in the sideyard, took the suitcase from the station wagon, and put it down before knocking on the enclosed back-porch door.

"Who's out there? What do you want?"

"It's Ken Svederup, about the snapshot."

Jessica came out onto the porch, unlocked the door, and invited me into the kitchen. The kitchen smelled of freshly perked coffee. There was a coffee cup and saucer on the table; also a chocolate-iced cake, a bowl of potato salad, ripe olives, jellied chicken, blue cheese crackers, a quartered dill pickle, a plate of the kind of weiners served on toothpicks at cocktail parties.

"I always say a midnight snack helps me to sleep better," said Jessica. Her appearance suggested she had caught up on sleep since the afternoon.

"It looks good to a man who missed out on dinner tonight."

"Sit down, Mr. Svederup, and help yourself. I always so enjoy seeing a man with a man's appetite."

I sat down and speared one of the minor-league weiners. Jessica brought cup and saucer. She produced the snapshot from her apron pocket.

"This is Babe?"

"That's Babe."

As a photographer, I could not give the snapshot much. A young woman whose eyes had blinked just as the shutter clicked posed in a doorway. The picture had been taken in reddish late afternoon sunlight, on a cheap film of the kind that renders red tones black. However, it was either a low-down door-knob, or she was a tall girl.

"She's about the right height," I said.

Jessica looked startled.

"I don't see any reason for calling her a chippy, though."

"She *acted* like a chippy. According to Ralph. Drinking at bars and picking up men while he was on the road."

"What road?"

"He drove a moving van for a living."

"I thought he drove a bread truck in St. Louis. The moving van job was in Oregon, wasn't it?"

"He may have married Babe out in Oregon for all I know."

"Well, is she in Oregon or Denver or St. Louis or Minneapolis right now?"

Jessica brought the percolator. She ran an even stream into my cup. "You ought to run for sheriff at the next election. You'd make a good one."

"I peek in mailboxes."

Jessica replaced the percolator on the stove. She came to the table, sat down, and helped herself to a slice of jellied chicken.

"I didn't give you an entirely complete or frank impression," she said. "There were things I did not feel free to bring out in front of Swede. I admit I wrote a letter to Babe and the St. Looie post office re-turned it to me."

"Why did you write to her?"

Jessica ate an olive and spat out the pit. "*She* wrote first. Trying to chisel money out of Ralph."

I must have looked incredulous.

"Mr. Svederup, you try living with it the way I did all these years. Knowing any minute the door can open and let in a woman to ruin your life. I was expecting her, and Ralph was expecting her." Jessica's heavy face took on a wild gypsy expression. "We had talked it over, and Ralph hated and loathed the ground she walked on, so much so he said he would see Babe dead before he'd give her a dime, and he meant it."

"Is that what you said in the letter?"

"Yes. I warned her to stay away from Ralph or he would put her to sleep as sure as God made green apples. I hoped to keep her from making a murderer of him."

She forked into the potato salad.

"I'd enjoy reading that letter," I said.

"I gave it to Mr. Burch. And I told him my suspicions."

"What do you suspect?"

"It's my opinion Babe teamed up with another man, and her and the man came here to Milquevais and killed Ralph and later on Babe will show up to claim the money from the bank."

"Why'd they kidnap you—leave you and Ralph's body in Larksdale?"

The heavy face hardened with peasant craftiness. "To clear themselves. Try and tie us in with Gladys' death."

"You're half-right, half-wrong."

She stared.

"Babe will show up, but it won't be to claim the money." I stood, stepped out through the porch, and returned with the suitcase.

Jessica was gone from the table.

A moment later, I heard her voice calling.

"I'm getting us some ice cream out of the freezer to go with our cake."

By the time I reached the head of the basement stairs, Jessica was halfway down the steps. It seemed likely she had got a slimpse of the suitcase. I followed her down the stairs.

The same rug carpeted the basement floor. She crossed it with powerful, purposeful steps. The same Indian clubs, minus one, stood against the wall. She did not glance at them. I assumed the missing club had gone into Lebijohn's trenchcoat pocket.

"Vanilla or choc'late?" she asked.

"You make the choice."

Jessica raised the freezer's thick lid. The lid was a full six feet in length, a yard in width, and covered on the lower side with thick frost that looked as if an unsuccessful effort had been made to break away a part of it.

Jessica bent over, and after a moment straightened. "Well, the carton's stuck fast. Can you get it loose for me, Mr. Svederup?"

At her side, I peered down into the freezer chest. It was a big one, full of goodies—wrapped beef, vegetables in store wrap, fruit packs, quarts on top of quarts of ice cream.

"The vanilla—that one."

I bent over.

She brought the freezer top down onto my shoulders.

It felt like being slugged on the spine with a sledge hammer. It doubled me up, face down in the goodies. Half of the breath jarred out of my lungs.

I didn't make the mistake of trying to inhale the lost breath. I braced my arms inside the chest, braced my legs outside, and bucked like a broncho.

The chest top heaved up with Jessica hanging onto it, trying to lay the weight of her big body onto it.

She saw I was out, though.

So she backed away, stumbled across the rug, and sat down on the basement steps. She moved as if her bones had again turned into lead. She began to cry big tears.

I hunted in my pockets and found a pad of matches. I lifted the lid, and lowered a lighted match into the interior. The match went out.

Ralph Riker had never got around to repairing the freezer motor. The goodies had been kept chilled with dry ice. Dry ice is carbon dioxide. The chest was a death chamber loaded with the heavier-than-air gas.

I lowered the coffin's lid and turned to lower the boom on Jessica. "That was attempted murder."

She may not have heard the words. Murder is a cracked mirror, a glass in which no one cares to recognize and acknowledge his own face.

"Poor Gladys. Was she down here doing reducing exercises in her bathing suit? Or washing her hair when you asked *her* to get something out of the freezer?"

She didn't want to talk about Gladys. So I said, "How could you have done it to a sweet, loving, harmless kid like Babe?"

That did it. She started telling me all over again how wrong I was about Babe. How that evening in the middle of last December she'd answered a knock at the front door:

"And in walked Babe, gussied up and war-painted like a whore, cool as cucumbers and bold as brass, smoking her cigarette and sprinkling the ashes around *my* front room. Saying she wanted to see *her* husband."

"Where was Ralph?"

"It happened to be bowling night."

"And Gladys?"

"Upstairs in her room, as usual—"

"What'd Babe want?"

"What do you suppose? Money, that's what. Claimed she'd been sick, she had to have an operation—the regulation hard-luck sob story."

"You threw her out?"

"How could I throw her out with Gladys upstairs and liable to hear?"

"You paid her money?"

"Where would I get it? Ralph believed in the man of the family handling the finances. I told Babe I would need a day or so. I talked her into going to the hotel, registering as Mrs. John Smith, and I'd phone her as soon as I raised the funds. And the next day I ran those checks through the machine, and I got Swede to sign them."

"He suspected nothing?"

"Later on he suspected plenty, but he wasn't in a position to say so much—" Jessica's mind wasn't with Swede Wolff. "The first damned thing Babe did was drift from the hotel down to the bowling alley. She got to talking to that windbag Heggland. She found out how Ralph was fixed, and she called me up to raise the price of her operation from twenty-five hundred to five thousand."

Now she looked squarely into my eyes. "Mr. Svederup, it's no use paying a penny to her kind of person. They always come back at you for more. And I couldn't go to the sheriff. Babe happened to be the legal wife, and the law wouldn't take into account she was a drunken, man-chasing floosie while I was always a respectable, hard-working helpmeet to Ralph."

Momentarily, a mirror image faced me. I saw myself in Tijauna, cursing the vagaries of Mexican law, and that was how Jessica felt about our law at home.

"So?"

"Mr. Svederup, I put a hammer and an axe in the car. I picked up Babe in front of the hotel. I let on I had the money at the Co-op and was going to put her on the train. Instead, I hit her over the head with the hammer, and then I drove home and cleaned up the terrible mess of blood in the car, and that night, after

Ralph was asleep, I drove out to Oak Lake and chopped a hole with the axe and sunk Babe and her suitcase."

You can understand murder only up to the point where the motives we all feel erupt into the sadistic savagery of which we're incapable.

"Why'd you keep her gloves?"

"The gloves were in her handbag, and the handbag wasn't heavy enough to sink—it took two bricks to sink the suitcase."

"Why'd you pick Oak Lake?"

"Well, you see, Babe had come to Milquevais on the train and stayed at the hotel and she had talked to Heggland. I thought Oak Lake was far enough away so nobody would make the connection if the body ever turned up."

I made a connection. I figured this was why she had made up the story about Gladys having a sister, and the sister coming to visit Gladys.

My mind searched for a way to sugar-coat the next question. I said, "I don't believe you wanted to hurt Gladys at all. She must have done something so you *had* to put her to sleep?"

"It was the damned computer's fault. The machine keeps a total of the checks issued, and the total has to square with the total of checks cashed. So even with Babe out of the picture, I still had to cash the checks or else explain why I ever issued them. And I could tell from Gladys' actions— She wasn't the type to accuse me to my face; she was going to say it behind my back. Quit her job and leave this house and then tip off the board of directors or the county attorney. I could smell that she was up to something, and what else could it be?"

It could have been the fantasy about Helen Holadare killing Charles Irvine. In fact, it had been. But the guilty don't *always* flee when no man pursueth. They sometimes rub out a bystander who seems to be looking their way.

Jessica stared at the freezer—reproachfully, I thought. Was she thinking I should have been dead in it before now, on a spasm of the glottis and paralysis of the respiratory system?

"I didn't get off so easy that time, either," she said. "Gladys wasn't in there long enough, or the gas wasn't strong enough. She'd started coming to by the time I got her to the car. I had to close the shed doors and run the motor with her in the luggage compartment."

She didn't get off so easy? How did she think Gladys felt, locked up in blackness and choking on the hot exhaust fumes? Jessica didn't give a damn about Gladys' sufferings, about Babe, or Ralph; she was off in an orbit through her own empty inner space.

"Ralph wasn't a bit of help to you, was he?" I said. I succeeded in sounding at least half-sympathetic.

"I think he knew Babe was in town—Heggland could have kidded him about a tall blonde chippy. Ralph knew from Staples about the car on the lake. I believe he took it into his head that Gladys wasn't the only body under the ice. I'm sure he bailed Staples out of jail and paid him to go fishing for Babe's remains. Why else would Staples phone to say he found the suitcase?"

I studied her. She was Jessica Clinton, the well-digger's daughter who'd graduated from Milquevais High School, who'd gone to business college, who'd worked awhile in the Cities and come home with a man supposed to be her husband.

"Did you think Ralph still had a yen for Babe? Is that why you killed her?" But she seemed to be thinking of something else. I asked, "And you thought Ralph would turn you in for killing her?"

It could have been he realized Jessica would have just as soon framed him for that rap.

It could have been all these things.

But what stuck in my craw was the last meal she ever cooked for Ralph—the hash and the peas out of a can for this guy who wanted the best of everything on the table. She had been too tight to prepare a decent dinner for a man she knew wouldn't live to eat it.

"The main thing was the money, wasn't it?"

Jessica answered from a far swing of her orbit in inner space. "I never understood Ralph. He was a floater; he didn't have a nickel laid up until I took him in hand. I'm the one that made him amount to something. I showed him what it's like to have funds in the bank, taught him the joys of saving and seeing the wealth grow." She had made an investment in acquiring and training a good provider.

Her eyes rounded at me pathetically. "And look at the thanks I got. Ralph would have turned me in for Babe and Gladys both, and stuck the reward in his pocket. He'd changed along the way so all he cared a hoot in hell for was the Almighty Dollar."

NINETEEN

Kelly greeted me: "You're late."

This was the next Tuesday night.

"Big day," I explained. "Lots of news."

Kelly wasn't listening. Clad in a colorful but shapeless Hawaiian Mother Hubbard called a "moo-moo," she crossed the living room and switched off the Late Show.

"The Busch brothers found Babe Riker's body in Oak Lake today," I said into the silence.

Kelly raised a hand and adjusted her toast-brown hair. She replied absently, "There's a letter from my mother on the kitchen table."

I said, "And they found a brokerage account of Gladys Irvine's, only she had it in the name of Gladys Holadare. She was buying Holadare Company shares under the counter. So that explains what became of her savings."

"I'll get you a bottle of beer from the icebox while you read mother's letter." The moo-moo whispered as Kelly stepped past me into the kitchen. I followed.

"The brokerage account sheds light on Gladys' psychology," I said. "She became obsessed with the Irvine-Holadare thing, just as people become obsessed with proving Shakespeare wasn't Shakespeare. Even her physical metabolism was involved. As her hopes grew, her body slimmed. When her hopes sank, her weight went up." I tugged on the dropcord bulb and sat down at the table. Mother Kelly's letter lay before me in an airmail envelope.

"Gladys lived on a teeter-totter," I continued. "Belief in her theory made her happy, serene, at peace with herself. Doubt made her gloomy, depressed, withdrawn. According to Jessica, the last weeks of December found Gladys in a disturbed, secretive, troubled mood. To me, that means Gladys was preyed on by doubts—that she acted under pressure from Dirk Lebijohn."

Kelly placed a bottle of Grain Belt and a glass before me.

I said, "Of course, Lebijohn was in cahoots with Willie Popke. They both knew Ed Horace was the real Charles Holadare."

Kelly nodded absently. She was the same pretty girl I'd married, only she seemed to be off in an orbit in her own inner space.

"You aren't listening to me," I said.

"You aren't reading mother's letter, either," Kelly said. "She writes that Roy Elling is out of jail. His bail was reduced to eight hundred dollars."

I stared at her. Her eyes were toast-brown with resentment.

"All the ones who didn't rush to put up sixteen hundred are being let out for eight now," she said.

"Forget it. It's only money. I haven't told you the really big news yet."

I reached into my pocket, got out the certified

check that Walter Burch had tonight written out payable to Kenneth Svederup. I spread it on top of Mother Kelly's airmail envelope.

Kelly said blankly, "It's still good in spite of Mrs. Holadare—?"

"Helen Holadare didn't offer the reward personally. The Holadare Company offered it, technically. It's still good."

Kelly sat looking at the check. "My God! Five thousand dollars." Her eyes brightened. She suddenly laughed. She said happily, "We can make the down payment on a house. We can furnish the house. We can take a trip—"

"It comes on top of my salary. It's all taxable, no deductions. After Federal and state income taxes, we're actually only thirty-five hundred ahead."

"Oh."

"And there's the thousand I borrowed from Old Man Crossway. We're ahead twenty-five hundred."

"Uh?"

"There's the nine hundred I took out of the bank. Actually we've gained sixteen hundred."

"Good grief!" cried Kelly. She started pacing the kitchen. The moo-moo whispered. Kelly's voice was barely louder than a whisper: "What's the matter with us? You walk in here with five thousand dollars, and in five minutes we've frittered away two-thirds of it. And what have we got to show for the money?"

I poured some beer into the glass. "Or you can look at it this way," I said. "We can pay the Old Man back at fifteen a week. We have thirty-five hundred in cash, enough to make the down payment and buy the furniture."

Kelly stopped pacing. Out of a brown study she said, "Maybe we shouldn't. It'd be nice to have a nest egg in the bank, too. We could just leave it there and watch the interest grow—"

I saw a mirror and faces in the mirror. The glass slipped from my fingers; the beer spilled an amber foaming pool over the table. I jumped up. "We're not that kind!"

Kelly reached across the table. She rescued the check and dried it on the moo-moo skirt. Then she came around the table.

"We've been turning into that kind, both of us, and I'm scared—" She wasn't scared. Her eyes flashed, and her lips smiled. "I'm not so crazy to build a house and settle down for the rest of our days in Milquevais. So why don't you quit the courthouse beat, and we'll take off for an island somewhere. We'll live on this check while you finish your book."

www.ingramcontent.com/pod-product-compliance
Lightning Source LLC
Chambersburg PA
CBHW020444270626
47155CB00022B/1371